Colby Utterback

Finding His Place

Colby Utterback

Finding His Place

A Novel

by

Jackie L. Smith

Copyright Page

Colby Utterback: Finding His Place

Published by Jackie L. Smith

Staffordsville, Kentucky

First Edition

Cover design by: Jessica Stacey

ISBN: 979-8-9959280-7-2 (paperback)

Printed in the United States of America

Dedication

For the kid in the back of the room
who thinks nobody sees him.

Somebody does.
"The world breaks everyone,
and afterward, many are strong
at the broken places."

— Ernest Hemingway

Table of Contents

Chapter One- The Weight

The first thing Colby Utterback did every morning was count heads.

He stood in the doorway of the bedroom he shared with Austin and Justin and looked across the narrow hallway to the girls' room, where Mary and Shirley slept in a bunk bed that leaned two inches to the left because one of the feet was a folded piece of cardboard instead of wood. Then he walked to the living room, where Carl was curled on the couch under a blanket that used to be blue and was now the color of nothing, his thumb in his mouth, his breath steady and slow.

Five. All five. All breathing. All here.

He didn't know when the counting had started. Sometime after Arnold left, maybe. Or sometime before — back when Arnold was still in the house and the counting was a different kind of check, not to see if they were breathing but to see if they were hurt. Those mornings had a different weight to them. Those mornings Colby would stand in the hallway and listen for crying, and if he didn't hear any he would let himself breathe, and if he did he would go to the sound and fix whatever needed fixing before his mother woke up.

Arnold had been gone for eight months. The restraining order was a piece of paper in a kitchen drawer, filed between an unpaid electric bill and a coupon for laundry detergent. Colby didn't trust the paper. Paper didn't stop a man who had grabbed a fifteen-year-old by the throat and beaten him until blood ran down his shirt and pooled on the kitchen floor. Paper didn't stop a man who had blackened both of a boy's eyes and broken his nose and then sat on the couch and opened another beer while the boy lay on the floor trying to remember how to breathe.

Paper was paper. Arnold was Arnold. And eight months was not enough time to stop counting heads.

Corbin, Idaho was the kind of town that people drove through on the way to somewhere else.

It sat in a valley between two ridges of pine-covered mountains, a main street with a hardware store and a diner and a post office and a grocery store, surrounded by blocks of houses that got smaller and older the farther you got from the center. The mountains were beautiful. Everyone said so — the tourists passing through in their SUVs, the hikers heading to the trailheads, the people on the internet who posted pictures of Idaho sunsets and wrote captions about God's country. The mountains were beautiful and the sky was big and the air was clean and none of it mattered when you were fifteen years old and your shoes had holes in them and your jacket was from the Goodwill bin and the boys at school could smell poverty the way dogs smell fear.

Colby walked to school because the bus didn't come to his street. The walk was a mile and a quarter, down Spruce to Main, past L&M Food Center where he worked four evenings a week, past the diner where he couldn't afford to eat, across the railroad tracks that divided the town into the side that had things and the side that didn't. Colby lived on the side that didn't.

The house was a rental — three bedrooms, one bathroom, a kitchen with a stove that only worked on two burners, and a living room where Carl slept because there was no room anywhere else. The landlord was a man named Petchek who came by on the first of the month and stood on the porch and waited for Wanda to bring the rent, and if the rent was late — which it was, every month, by at least three days — Petchek would stand on the porch a little longer and look at the house with the expression of a man calculating whether the trouble of eviction was worth the trouble of finding a new tenant who would also be late.

Wanda always found the money. Colby didn't know how. She worked days at the laundromat on Fifth Street, folding other people's clothes for eleven dollars an hour, and the math of eleven dollars an hour and one income and six children and rent and food and electricity and the Goodwill bin for shoes and jackets did not add up to a life. It added up to a survival. And the difference between a life and a survival was the difference between breathing and living, and Colby Utterback, at fifteen years old, understood that difference better than most people three times his age.

School was a building he went to because the law said he had to.

Corbin High School. Two hundred and forty students. One hallway. Lockers that stuck in winter because the heating system couldn't keep up with the cold that seeped through the cinder block walls. A gym that smelled like sweat and floor polish. A cafeteria where Colby ate the free lunch that was the only hot meal he could count on five days a week, sitting alone at a table by the window, because the window was something to look at when you had nobody to talk to.

The bullying had started in seventh grade and had never stopped.

It wasn't dramatic. It wasn't the kind of bullying you saw in movies, where a big kid shoved a small kid into a locker and the whole school watched and someone eventually stepped in. It was quieter than that. More patient. It was the daily accumulation of small cruelties delivered by boys who had learned that the kid in the Goodwill jacket with the bruises on his face wouldn't fight back, because the kid in the Goodwill jacket had been trained by a man with heavy hands to absorb pain without complaint.

Trent Haskell was the worst. He was sixteen, a year older than Colby, held back in eighth grade for reasons nobody discussed, with the build of a kid who had grown into his father's body before he'd grown into his father's brain. Trent didn't hit Colby — that would have been simple, and simple could be reported. Trent did something worse. He talked.

"Smells like the Utterbacks' house in here," he would say when Colby walked past. Not loud. Just loud enough. The boys around him would laugh — the obligatory laugh of kids who were glad it wasn't them and who maintained their safety by participating in someone else's humiliation.

"Hey Colby, your stepdad beat your mom yet today, or just you?"

"Utterback. Utter. Back. Like, go back to where you came from."

The words were small. Individual, they weighed nothing. But words accumulate the way snow accumulates — flake by flake, day by day, until the weight of them is enough to collapse a roof. Colby's roof was bending. He could feel it. The weight pressed down on him every morning when he walked through the front doors of Corbin High and lasted until he walked out the back doors at three o'clock, and by the time he reached L&M Food Center for his shift at four, the weight had settled into his shoulders and his chest and the place behind his eyes where the headaches lived.

His grades were falling. Not because he was stupid — Colby Utterback was not stupid, and the few teachers who paid attention knew it. Mrs. Navarro, who taught sophomore English, had pulled him aside in September and said, "Colby, your essay on To Kill a Mockingbird was the best in the class. What's happening?" And Colby had looked at her and wanted to say

everything and said "Nothing, ma'am" instead, because telling a teacher what was happening meant opening a door that he had spent his whole life learning to keep shut.

He worked the four o'clock to eight o'clock shift at L&M Food Center.

L&M was the only grocery store in Corbin. It sat on Main Street between the hardware store and the post office, a single-story building with a faded green awning and a parking lot that held twenty cars and was never full. The owner was a man named Lloyd Meeker — the L in L&M, the M being his wife Margie, who ran the register and called every customer "hon" and kept a jar of peppermints by the checkout that she refilled every morning from a bag she bought at Costco in Boise.

Colby was a stock boy. He unloaded trucks, stacked shelves, organized the storeroom, swept the floors, and did whatever else Lloyd needed done for eight dollars and fifty cents an hour, four hours a day, four days a week. The math was $136 a week before taxes. After taxes, it was closer to $115. He gave Wanda $80 and kept the rest for shoes and school supplies and the occasional bag of chips that he ate in the storeroom on his break, sitting on a crate of canned tomatoes, staring at the concrete wall, thinking about nothing because thinking about something was worse.

Lloyd was a decent man. He didn't ask Colby about the bruises that had been there in the early months. He didn't ask about the grades or the family or the shoes with the holes. He just put Colby to work and paid him on time and said "Good job, son" at the end of each shift, and the word "son" landed in Colby's chest every time like a stone dropping into a well — a long fall, a distant splash, an echo that lasted longer than it should have.

Colby didn't remember his real father. The man had left when Colby was three — a name on a birth certificate and a shape in a photograph that Wanda kept in a shoebox in her closet. He had never called. He had never written. He had never sent money or a birthday card or any sign that he remembered the son he'd left behind. Colby had stopped thinking about him years ago, the way a person stops looking for something they've accepted is lost.

Arnold had been the replacement. Wanda had married him when Colby was nine, and for the first year things had been better — a second income, a man in the house, the illusion of a family that worked. Then Arnold started drinking. Then the drinking started producing a different Arnold — louder, meaner, a man whose hands moved from the beer can to the belt to the back of Colby's head with increasing frequency and decreasing provocation. By the time Colby was twelve, the hitting was regular. By thirteen, it was expected. By fourteen, the night in the kitchen, the throat, the blood, the floor.

Uncle James had come the next morning. He'd taken one look at Colby's face and his own face had gone white and then red and then a color that Colby had never seen on a human being before — the color of a man whose anger was so large it had nowhere to go except into his jaw, which clamped shut so hard the muscles in his neck stood out like cables.

James had taken Colby to Judge Erhardt. The judge had looked at Colby's face and asked questions and written things down and said that charges could be filed if Wanda was willing to press them. James had driven to the house. He'd talked to Wanda in the kitchen for twenty minutes. Colby sat on the porch and listened to his uncle's voice rising and his mother's voice not rising, staying low, staying flat, staying in the register of a woman who had calculated the math of prosecuting the man she was married to and had decided that the math didn't work.

Arnold would get out. Arnold would come back. Arnold would be worse.

Wanda didn't press charges. James left the house with the look of a man who had been defeated by a sister he loved and a system he couldn't fix. Arnold was gone within a month anyway — not because of the law, but because Wanda had finally, quietly, without announcement, changed the locks and put his things on the porch and told him through the closed door that if he came back she would call James, and James would not bring a judge.

Arnold left. The restraining order came later. And Colby was left with two black eyes that faded to yellow and then to nothing, and a broken nose that healed crooked, and the knowledge that the people who were supposed to protect him had done so only after the damage was done and in a way that required him to be damaged first.

He came home from L&M at 8:15 on a Wednesday evening in October.

The house was loud. It was always loud. Justin and Austin were fighting over the television remote. Shirley was sitting at the kitchen table doing homework with the concentration of a ten-year-old who had decided that schoolwork was the one thing in her life she could control.

Mary was in the girls' room with the door closed, which meant she was either reading or crying, and Colby had learned not to knock on Mary's door because thirteen-year-old girls needed a closed door the way fish needed water.

Carl was asleep on the couch. Thumb in mouth. Blanket that used to be blue.

Wanda was in the kitchen. She was sitting at the table across from Shirley, not eating, not reading, just sitting with a cup of coffee that Colby could tell from the doorway was cold, because his mother held hot coffee with both hands and cold coffee with one, and the hand that wasn't holding the cup was lying on the table palm-up, like it was waiting for something to be placed in it.

She looked tired. She always looked tired. But tonight the tiredness had a different quality — deeper, heavier, the tiredness of a woman who had been carrying a weight for so long that the weight had become part of her body and she could no longer tell where the exhaustion ended and she began.

"Hi, baby," Wanda said.

"Hi, Mom."

"How was work?"

"Fine. Lloyd says hi."

Lloyd had not said hi. Lloyd had said "Good job, son" and Colby had carried the word home like a coin in his pocket, and the coin was worth more than the $28.90 he'd earned in four hours of stacking shelves and sweeping floors.

He put $20 on the table next to Wanda's coffee cup. He did this every Wednesday — the midweek contribution, the money that bought milk and bread and the generic cereal that Carl ate by the fistful and the eggs that Wanda scrambled every morning for six children because eggs were cheap and filling and a mother's love could be measured in the things she put on the table when the table had no right to have anything on it.

Wanda looked at the twenty. She didn't pick it up. She looked at it and then she looked at Colby and her eyes did the thing they sometimes did — the thing that made Colby look away, because the thing in his mother's eyes was not sadness and was not gratitude. It was shame. The shame of a woman whose fifteen-year-old son was putting money on her table because she couldn't put enough there herself.

"Thank you, baby," Wanda said.

Colby nodded. He went to the kitchen and made himself a peanut butter sandwich and ate it standing at the counter and drank a glass of water and washed the knife and the glass and put them away. He checked on Carl — still sleeping, still breathing, thumb still in mouth. He told Justin and Austin to stop fighting and go to bed. He knocked on Mary's door and said "Goodnight" and heard "Goodnight" come back, steady and dry, which meant reading, not crying.

He went to his room. He lay on his bed in the dark. Austin was already asleep on the lower bunk. Justin was curled on the mattress on the floor, his blanket pulled over his head, making the small sounds of a six-year-old falling asleep.

Colby stared at the ceiling. The ceiling had a water stain shaped like a hand. He had been staring at that stain for three years, ever since they moved into this house, and the stain had not changed and neither had anything else.

He thought about tomorrow. School. Trent. The hallway. The words. The cafeteria. The window. Then L&M. The shelves. The storeroom. Lloyd's "Good job, son." Then home. The heads. The counting. The twenty on the table. The shame in his mother's eyes.

The same day, over and over, with nothing at the end of it except another day exactly like it.

He closed his eyes. He didn't pray. He had stopped praying the night Arnold grabbed him by the throat, because a God who let that happen to a kid wasn't a God who was listening. He just lay in the dark and waited for sleep, the way he waited for everything — patiently, without expectation, the way a person waits at a bus stop when they're not sure the bus is still running.

Tomorrow was Thursday. He had school and then a shift at L&M. Lloyd had asked him to organize the back of the storeroom — the deep part, behind the pallets of dog food and the cases of bottled water, where nobody had gone in months and the inventory was a mess.

Colby didn't know it yet, but tomorrow was the last ordinary day of his life.

Chapter Two - The Last Ordinary Day

Carl's thumb was out.

That was the first thing Colby saw when he walked into the living room — not the wheezing, which he heard a second later, but the thumb. Carl's thumb was always in his mouth. Sleeping, waking, sitting on the couch, riding on Wanda's hip — the thumb was a permanent fixture, as constant as the blanket that used to be blue. When the thumb was in, Carl was okay. When the thumb was out, something was wrong.

The thumb was out. It hung at Carl's side, wet with spit, and his mouth was open, pulling air in shallow gasps, and the sound coming from his chest was the thin, high-pitched whistle that Colby knew the way he knew his own heartbeat — the sound of airways that had decided to narrow in the night. Colby was across the room in four steps, bare feet on cold linoleum, kneeling beside the couch where his four-year-old brother lay with his small chest rising and falling in the labored rhythm of a bellows that wouldn't open all the way.

"Easy, buddy," Colby said to Carl. He kept his voice low and steady, the way he'd learned to do. Panic made asthma worse. Colby had read that on a library computer in seventh grade, the first time Carl had turned blue in his arms, and he had never forgotten it. Calm voice. Slow hands. Get the inhaler.

The inhaler was on the windowsill above the couch. Colby picked it up, shook it twice, and held it to Carl's lips. Carl's eyes were open now — wide, frightened, the eyes of a child who couldn't get enough air and didn't understand why his body was doing this to him.

"Breathe in when I press it," Colby told Carl. "Big breath. Like blowing up a balloon, but backwards."

Carl breathed. Colby pressed. The inhaler hissed. Carl's chest expanded, held, released. The whistle thinned. Didn't disappear, but thinned, the way a siren thins as it moves away from you.

"One more," Colby said to Carl. "You're doing good."

The second puff went in. Carl's breathing steadied. The whistle faded to a rasp, and the rasp faded to something close to normal, and the fear in Carl's eyes dimmed to the confusion of a child who had been pulled out of sleep by his own lungs and didn't know what day it was.

Colby sat on the floor beside the couch. He put his hand on Carl's chest and felt it rise and fall, rise and fall, steady now, the rhythm of a body that had been reminded how to breathe. Carl's eyes drifted shut. His hand came up, slowly, and the thumb found his mouth and slid in — the reflex of a child returning to the one comfort his body trusted. Thumb in. Carl was okay.

Colby stayed on the floor. He counted Carl's breaths the way he counted heads — automatically, without thinking, a habit built from fear. Ten breaths. Twenty. All clear. All steady.

The inhaler was almost empty. He shook it again and felt the lightness of a canister that had maybe ten puffs left, and the math of that settled into his chest the way all the math of this family settled into his chest — heavily, quietly, with the weight of a problem that had no solution he could afford. A new inhaler without insurance was over three hundred dollars. With the clinic discount Wanda sometimes got, it was sixty. Sixty dollars was almost half his weekly pay. Sixty dollars was the difference between Petchek getting the rent on time and Petchek standing on the porch three extra days with the expression of a man calculating eviction.

He set the inhaler back on the windowsill. He stood up. He counted heads.

Carl on the couch. Breathing.

He crossed the hallway. Austin and Justin were tangled in their bunks, Austin's arm hanging over the side of the lower bed, Justin curled on the mattress on the floor with his blanket pulled over his face. Colby pulled the blanket down so Justin could breathe. The kid slept like he was hiding, even in sleep, even eight months after the man he was hiding from was gone.

Girls' room. Mary was already awake, sitting on the top bunk reading a paperback in the gray light that came through the window. She looked at Colby in the doorway and raised her eyebrows, and the eyebrows were a question — the same question she asked with her face every morning without saying a word.

"Carl had an episode," Colby said to Mary. "He's okay now. Inhaler's almost out."

Mary nodded. She didn't say anything. At thirteen, Mary Utterback had learned that some information didn't need a response — it needed to be filed and carried, and she carried it the way Colby carried everything, silently, in the place behind her eyes where the family's problems lived.

Shirley was still asleep on the bottom bunk, her homework folder clutched to her chest like a stuffed animal.

Five. All five. All breathing. Thursday.

Wanda was in the kitchen.

She was scrambling eggs on the two burners that worked, moving the spatula with the mechanical efficiency of a woman who had performed this action six thousand times and could do it with her eyes closed. The eggs were from a flat she bought at the discount grocery in Boise once a month

— thirty eggs for four dollars, which worked out to just over thirteen cents per egg, and Wanda could feed six children on eight eggs and toast and still have enough left for tomorrow.

The kids ate breakfast at home because Wanda made sure of it. But the real meal — the meal Wanda depended on — happened at school. All five school-age children qualified for free breakfast and free lunch through the federal program, and those two meals were the architecture of the family's survival. Ten free meals a day, five days a week. Without them, the math didn't work. Without them, eggs and toast weren't enough, and Colby's $115 a week wasn't enough, and eleven dollars an hour wasn't enough, and the whole structure would collapse like a house of cards in a draft.

Wanda didn't talk about it. She never said the words "free lunch" out loud, the same way she never said the words "food stamps" or "clinic discount" or "past due." The words existed in the kitchen drawer with the restraining order and the unpaid electric bill, filed under the heading of things that were true and shameful and necessary.

"Carl had a bad morning," Colby said to Wanda. He poured himself a glass of water from the tap. Coffee was for Wanda. There was no second cup.

Wanda's spatula stopped. She didn't turn around. The spatula just stopped, mid-scrape, and the eggs sat in the pan and the kitchen was quiet for a moment — the quiet of a mother hearing the name of her youngest child and the word "bad" in the same sentence.

"How bad?" Wanda asked Colby, still facing the stove.

"Wheezing. I gave him two puffs. He's sleeping now." Colby paused. "Inhaler's almost empty, Mom."

Wanda's shoulders tightened. The tightening was small — a quarter-inch lift, a compression of the muscles between her shoulder blades — but Colby saw it because he had spent fifteen years reading his mother's body the way a sailor reads the sky. That particular tightening meant money. It meant another bill that couldn't be paid without unpaying something else. It meant the math again, always the math, the math that never added up and never would.

"I'll call the clinic," Wanda said to Colby. She started scraping the eggs again. The motion was harder now, faster, the spatula hitting the pan with the rhythm of a woman whose hands were angry because the rest of her couldn't afford to be.

Colby wanted to say he'd pay for it. He wanted to take the sixty dollars from his pocket and put it on the counter the way he put the twenty on the table every Wednesday. But sixty dollars was three days of work, and the rent was due in nine days, and if he gave Wanda sixty dollars for the inhaler she'd be short on rent, and if she was short on rent Petchek would stand on the porch, and if Petchek stood on the porch long enough he'd stop standing and start filing.

So Colby drank his water and said nothing, because the math of this family was a locked room with no doors, and every time he thought he'd found a way out he discovered it was just another wall with a window painted on it.

Mary had the younger kids ready by 7:15.

She stood at the front door like a drill sergeant who happened to be thirteen years old and five foot two, checking shoes and backpacks and faces for evidence of syrup or toothpaste or the particular chaos that four children under the age of ten could produce in twenty minutes of morning routine.

"Shirley, zip your jacket," Mary said. "Austin, where's your homework folder? Justin, stop picking your nose."

Justin stopped picking his nose. Austin found his homework folder under the couch. Shirley zipped her jacket with the concentrated care of a child who had been told once and would not need to be told again.

Mary walked them to school every morning — Shirley and Austin to Corbin Elementary, Justin to the primary wing on the other side of the same building. The walk was six blocks. Mary covered it in twelve minutes, delivered the children to their respective doors, and then walked another four blocks to Corbin Middle School, where she arrived exactly on time, every day, without fail, because Mary Utterback had decided at some point in her thirteen years that reliability was the one currency she could earn without a job.

Wanda left twenty minutes after the kids, Carl on her hip, his inhaler in her pocket, a coloring book and a box of crayons in the bag that hung from her shoulder next to her purse. Carl spent his days at the laundromat on Fifth Street, sitting on a folding chair behind the counter, drawing pictures of things that a four-year-old found important — trucks, dogs, houses with too many windows, the sun with a face. The chair was next to the dryer vent, which kept it warm, and the hum of the machines put Carl to sleep most afternoons, which meant his lungs got the rest they needed and Wanda got the quiet she needed to fold two hundred pounds of other people's clothes without breaking down.

Colby left last. He locked the front door — the deadbolt that Wanda had installed herself with a YouTube video and a drill borrowed from Uncle James — and walked to school alone. His route was different from Mary's. Longer. Down Spruce to Main, past L&M, past the diner, across the tracks. The walk took twenty-two minutes. Colby had timed it once and never bothered timing it again, because nothing about the walk ever changed. The same houses. The same cracked sidewalks. The same mountains on either side of the valley, beautiful and useless and permanent.

Trent Haskell was waiting.

Not literally waiting. Trent Haskell did not wake up in the morning and position himself at the front entrance of Corbin High School for the specific purpose of tormenting Colby Utterback. It was worse than that. Trent was just there — leaning against the brick wall by the double doors with two boys from the wrestling team, a Styrofoam cup of gas station coffee in his hand, his letterman jacket open despite the October cold because boys like Trent Haskell did not zip their jackets. Zipping was for people who admitted the cold affected them, and Trent did not admit that anything affected him, because admitting was weakness, and weakness was the thing you identified in other people and used against them.

Colby walked past with his head down. It didn't matter. It never mattered. Head down, head up, other side of the hallway, different entrance — none of it mattered because Trent's radar was tuned to Colby's frequency, and nothing Colby did could change the frequency.

"Utterback," Trent said. Not shouting. Conversational. The way a person says the name of someone they've claimed ownership of.

Colby kept walking. Through the doors. Into the hallway. The lockers, the cinder block, the smell of floor polish and cheap heating.

"Hey, I'm talking to you, Utterback." Trent's voice was behind him now, closer, and one of the wrestling boys laughed — the short, sharp laugh of an audience member who knows the show is about to start.

Colby stopped. He stopped because stopping was easier than not stopping. Because not stopping meant Trent would follow, and Trent following meant the performance would last longer and draw a bigger crowd, and a bigger crowd meant more witnesses to whatever Trent decided to say, and more witnesses meant more people who would look at Colby Utterback and see the kid who got picked on and did nothing about it.

He turned. He looked at Trent. Trent was smiling. It was not a smile that had anything to do with happiness.

"Smelled your jacket from outside," Trent said to Colby. "What is that, Goodwill? Or is that just the natural Utterback smell?"

The wrestling boys laughed. A girl passing by glanced at Colby and looked away fast — the look-away of someone who recognized cruelty and wanted no part of it and also wanted no part of stopping it.

Colby said nothing. He turned and walked to his locker, and the silence he carried with him was not the silence of a boy who had nothing to say. It was the silence of a boy who had been taught by a man with heavy hands that speaking up got you hit, and the lesson had lasted longer than the man.

He sat through first period. Second period. Third. The day moved the way school days moved for Colby — slowly, in the margins, the way a person moves through a room full of furniture they're trying not to bump into. He answered when teachers called on him. He took notes. He ate the free lunch in the cafeteria at the table by the window, alone, the meatloaf and mashed potatoes and carton of milk that were the best meal of his day, paid for by a government program that existed because someone in Washington had once calculated the cost of feeding a poor kid versus the cost of not feeding him and had decided that feeding was cheaper.

He thought about Carl. The wheezing. The inhaler. The sixty dollars. He thought about Wanda's shoulders tightening and the eggs hitting the pan harder and the sound of a woman's anger coming through a spatula because it had nowhere else to go.

He thought about the ceiling stain shaped like a hand. He thought about the same day, over and over. He thought about the bus stop where you wait for a bus that might not be running.

And then the thought came. It came the way it always came — not as a decision, not as a plan, but as a door at the end of a long hallway. A door that was always there. A door that Colby had walked past a hundred times and never opened, but whose handle he sometimes touched, just to feel the cold metal, just to know it was still an option.

What if I wasn't here.

Not a question. Not even a sentence. A shape in the dark, the outline of a thought that had no detail and no plan and no intention behind it. Just the shape. Just the idea that the world contained an exit, and the exit was always available, and knowing it was available was sometimes the only thing that made the hallway bearable.

He didn't dwell on it. He never dwelled on it. The thought came and he acknowledged it the way he acknowledged the cold in his jacket and the ache behind his eyes and the sound of Trent's voice in the hallway — as a fact of his life that existed alongside all the other facts, neither larger nor smaller, just present.

And then the bell rang, and the day moved on, and Colby moved with it, because the other fact of his life — the fact that outweighed the door at the end of the hallway — was five heads that needed counting. A mother who needed $80 on the table. A four-year-old on a couch who needed someone to listen for his breathing in the dark.

He couldn't open the door. They needed him. And being needed was not the same as being wanted, but it was enough to keep him in the hallway.

He clocked in at L&M at four o'clock.

Lloyd was at the register. Margie had gone home early — a dentist appointment, Lloyd said, which meant Lloyd was running the front alone, which meant Colby would handle the stocking and the storeroom without supervision, which was fine because Colby had been doing this job for seven months and knew the store better than most of the products knew themselves.

"Colby, I need the back organized," Lloyd said to Colby from behind the register. "The deep end. Past the pallets. Stuff back there hasn't been touched since spring. Christmas inventory's coming in three weeks and I need that space clear."

"Yes, sir," Colby said to Lloyd.

"Take your time with it. Do it right." Lloyd paused. He looked at Colby over the top of his reading glasses — the bifocals he wore on a chain around his neck like a man who had accepted that age was winning and had decided to accessorize the defeat. "You okay today, son?"

The word again. Son. The stone in the well.

"I'm fine, Mr. Meeker," Colby said to Lloyd.

Lloyd held the look for a half-second longer than necessary. Lloyd Meeker was not a man who pried. He was a man who noticed. He noticed the dark circles under Colby's eyes. He noticed the jacket that was too thin for October. He noticed the way the boy's shoulders pulled in when the bell above the front door rang, as if loud sounds triggered something in him that had nothing to do with groceries. Lloyd noticed all of it and said none of it, because Lloyd Meeker had learned long ago that some kids didn't need someone to ask questions. They needed someone to say "Good job, son" and mean it.

"All right," Lloyd said to Colby. "Holler if you need anything."

Colby went to the storeroom.

The storeroom was the back third of L&M Food Center.

It ran the full width of the building, a low-ceilinged concrete room with fluorescent lights that buzzed and flickered and cast everything in a pale, greenish glow that made even new products look old. The front of the storeroom was organized — pallets of dog food on the left, cases of bottled water on the right, a center aisle wide enough for a hand truck. The shelving along both walls held overstock, seasonal items, and the kind of products that small grocery stores ordered once and never reordered because nobody in Corbin, Idaho wanted them.

The front Colby knew. The front was his territory — four evenings a week of stacking and sorting and sweeping.

The back was different.

The deep end of the storeroom was a place where order had gone to die. Past the pallets, past the bottled water, past the point where the fluorescent lights gave way to a single bulb on a pull chain, the room narrowed and the clutter thickened and the air changed — cooler, denser, carrying the smell of cardboard and dust and something underneath that Colby couldn't identify. Something mineral. Something old.

Colby pulled the chain. The bulb came on, a dim yellow circle that reached maybe ten feet in any direction before giving up. Beyond its reach, the storeroom receded into shadow.

He started working.

The first hour was straightforward. He moved boxes, read labels, sorted inventory. Cases of canned goods that had been shoved back here in March. A pallet of paper towels still in the shrink wrap. Holiday decorations from last year — a cardboard display for Valentine's candy, a string of plastic Easter eggs, a faded poster for the Fourth of July that said CELEBRATE FREEDOM in red, white, and blue letters that had been white once and were now the color of dust.

He stacked, sorted, cleared. The work was good. The work was always good. Physical labor asked nothing of Colby except his body, and his body knew how to do things his mind couldn't — move, lift, carry, stack. The body didn't think about Trent or Carl or the inhaler or the door at the end of the hallway. The body just worked, and the working was a kind of silence, and the silence was a kind of peace.

He pushed deeper.

Past the holiday displays. Past a shelf of cleaning supplies that Lloyd had probably forgotten existed. Past a stack of flattened cardboard boxes leaning against the wall like tired soldiers. The storeroom was longer than it looked from the front — the building extended farther back than the retail space suggested, and the deep end was a place that existed in the permanent twilight of neglect, where things went and stayed and were forgotten.

The single bulb was behind him now. He was working by the light of his phone, propped on a shelf, casting a white rectangle into the dark. The air was cooler back here. Noticeably cooler. The smell was stronger too — the mineral smell, the underground smell, the smell of earth and stone and time.

He moved a stack of boxes. Behind the boxes was another stack. Behind that stack was a gap — a space between the shelving and the far wall, maybe two feet wide, packed with old inventory that had been shoved back there and abandoned. Colby could see the wall behind it, or what he thought was the wall — a surface darker than the rest, slightly uneven, as if the concrete had been poured over something that wasn't flat.

He squeezed into the gap. He needed to get to the wall to see what was behind the last row of boxes. Lloyd wanted the space cleared, and the space wouldn't be clear until everything was accounted for and either moved or thrown out.

He pushed a box of outdated cereal aside. He stepped forward. His foot came down on the concrete floor, and the floor was solid, and normal, and then he pushed past the last shelf and took another step and his foot came down on something that was not concrete.

It was dirt.

Soft, dry, packed earth. The kind of ground you'd find in a forest. The kind of ground that had never seen concrete.

Colby looked down. He was standing on dirt. His left foot was on the concrete floor of L&M Food Center's storeroom, and his right foot was on bare ground, and between the two feet there was no line, no edge, no border. The concrete just ended and the dirt began, as if the building had been built on the edge of something and the something was still there, underneath, waiting.

He looked up.

The fluorescent light was gone. The shelf was gone. The boxes were gone. The storeroom wall that should have been two feet in front of him was not there. In its place was air — open, cool, moving air, carrying the smell of pine and wood smoke and wet earth and a sky that was not a ceiling.

He was standing at the edge of a clearing. The clearing was ringed with trees — enormous trees, taller than anything that grew in Corbin, their trunks as wide as cars, their branches woven into a canopy that filtered pale morning light into columns of gold and green. The ground was covered in leaves and moss. A creek ran somewhere to his left, the sound of water over stones. A bird called from somewhere in the canopy — not a bird he recognized, not a sound he'd heard before.

Colby turned around. Behind him was a wall of rock — a low outcropping, maybe six feet tall, covered in lichen, with a narrow gap at its base where the shelf and the boxes and the storeroom should have been. The gap was dark. It smelled like dust and cardboard and the faintest trace of floor polish. But it was a gap in a rock wall in a forest that shouldn't exist, and the storeroom was gone, and the fluorescent light was gone, and the phone he'd propped on the shelf was gone, and the only light was the pale gold filtering through a canopy of trees that were older than anything Colby Utterback had ever seen.

"The light was wrong. It had been evening in the storeroom — five o'clock, maybe later, the October sun already dropping behind the mountains. But the light coming through these trees was morning light, climbing, not falling. As if the day had reset. As if time had broken along with everything else."

He stood very still. His heart was beating fast. His hands were at his sides. His breath was coming in short, shallow pulls, the way his breath came when Arnold was in the house and the house was quiet and the quiet meant something bad was about to happen.

But this was not Arnold. This was not the house. This was something else entirely — something that Colby's brain could not process because his brain had no category for it, no file, no folder, no drawer in the kitchen of his mind where he could put the fact that he had taken a step in a grocery storeroom in Corbin, Idaho, and landed in a forest that smelled like a world before roads.

The creek. The birds. The trees.

The sky above the canopy, pale and wide and impossibly clean.

Colby Utterback, fifteen years old, stock boy, brother, counter of heads, carrier of weight, stood in the clearing and felt the first real silence of his life. Not the silence of a bedroom at night with brothers sleeping. Not the silence of a cafeteria table by the window. Not the silence of a boy who had been trained to be quiet.

This silence was different. This silence had nothing to do with absence. It was full — full of wind and water and the creak of branches and the hum of a world that was alive in a way that Corbin had never been alive, a way that had nothing to do with people and everything to do with the earth itself, breathing.

He didn't know where he was. He didn't know how he'd gotten here. He didn't know if he could get back.

But for the first time in longer than he could remember, the weight on his shoulders lifted. Not because the weight was gone. Because the world had gotten bigger, and in a bigger world, the same weight felt lighter.

He took a step. The leaves crunched under his sneakers. The forest stretched in every direction, deep and green and endless, and somewhere in the distance a column of smoke rose above the tree line — thin, steady, the smoke of a fire that someone was tending.

Colby walked toward it. He didn't know what else to do. He had spent fifteen years walking toward things he didn't understand — the next day, the next shift, the next morning of counting heads. This was no different. This was just another direction, and at the end of it was smoke, and smoke meant fire, and fire meant a person, and a person was better than standing alone in a forest that existed in a place where forests shouldn't be.

He walked. The trees closed behind him. The gap in the rock wall disappeared into the undergrowth, and the storeroom and the shelves and the fluorescent light and the life he'd been living became something behind him, and the forest and the smoke and whatever waited at the end of the walk became something ahead.

Thursday. The last ordinary day of his life.

It was over.

Chapter Three – Smoke

The forest had no paths.

Colby pushed through undergrowth that reached his waist — ferns, brambles, vines that grabbed his ankles and held on like hands. His sneakers were soaked. His L&M polo shirt was torn at the sleeve where a branch had caught it and pulled. His jeans were streaked with mud from a dip in the ground he hadn't seen until he was knee-deep in it, black water and dead leaves and the smell of rot rising around him like breath from a grave.

He kept walking. Toward the smoke. The smoke was the only thing in this place that suggested a human being, and a human being was the only thing Colby wanted to find, because everything else — the trees, the silence, the birds he didn't recognize, the sheer impossible size of this forest — was too large for his brain to hold. So he held onto the smoke instead, the thin gray line above the canopy, and he walked toward it the way a drowning person swims toward a light on the shore.

The forest went on and on. Not the forests he knew from the mountains around Corbin — those were managed forests, thinned by logging, crisscrossed with trails and fire roads, the kind of wilderness that had a parking lot at the edge of it. This forest had no edge. The trees were enormous — oaks and hickories and chestnuts with trunks wider than

Colby was tall, their canopy so thick that the sky was only visible in fragments, like blue glass in a green ceiling. The ground was soft with centuries of fallen leaves, layer upon layer, a carpet that gave under his feet and released the smell of earth and decay and something sweet that he couldn't name.

There were no power lines. No airplane contrails. No distant hum of highway traffic. No sounds that belonged to the world Colby had come from. Just birds, wind, water, and the creaking of branches that had been growing since before anyone he'd ever known had been born.

He walked for what felt like an hour. Maybe longer. He had no phone, no watch, no way to measure time except the angle of the light through the canopy, which was steeper now, more golden, which meant the sun was higher than when he'd arrived, which meant the morning was moving forward in whatever place this was, and time existed here even if nothing else made sense.

The smoke was closer. He could smell it now — wood smoke, hickory maybe, and underneath it something cooking. Meat. The smell of meat over a fire, and the smell hit his stomach before it hit his brain, because Colby Utterback had eaten a free school lunch and a peanut butter sandwich yesterday and nothing since, and his body recognized food the way a compass recognizes north.

He came through a stand of birch trees and the forest opened into a clearing.

The camp was small.

A lean-to built against a rock face — rough-cut poles lashed together with strips of bark, covered with animal hides that had been scraped and stretched and layered to keep out rain. A fire pit in front of it, ringed with stones, the fire burning low and steady, the kind of fire that had been tended through the night by someone who knew what they were doing. A spit over the fire held a piece of meat — a haunch of something, rabbit maybe, dark and glistening with fat that dripped and hissed on the coals.

Pelts hung from a rack made of branches. Five or six of them — beaver, deer, something dark and thick that might have been bear. They were stretched on wooden frames and tied with sinew, and the craftsmanship was rough but precise, the work of hands that had done this a thousand times.

Tools leaned against the rock face. A long rifle — not a modern rifle, not anything Colby had seen outside of a history textbook. It was made of dark wood and metal, with a flintlock mechanism and a barrel that was longer than Colby's arm. Next to it, a hatchet. A skinning knife in a leather sheath. A coil of rope that looked hand-twisted. A wooden bucket. A pair of moccasins drying near the fire.

Colby's brain did the math. It did the math the way it always did — automatically, without permission, the way it calculated rent and grocery money and how many puffs were left in Carl's inhaler. The math said: no plastic. No metal that wasn't hand-forged. No synthetic fabric. No zippers, no rubber, no glass. Everything in this camp was made of wood, leather, stone, bone, or hand-forged iron. Everything was made by hand or taken from an animal.

This was not a modern camp. This was not a reenactment or a hunting trip or a man who'd gone off the grid. This was something else. Something that the storeroom and the portal and the impossible forest had been building toward, and Colby's brain arrived at the conclusion the same way it arrived at every hard truth — quietly, reluctantly, with the resignation of a mind that had learned early that the world did not arrange itself for your comfort.

This is the past.

He didn't know how far back. He didn't know the year or the century. But the lean-to and the flintlock and the hand-scraped pelts and the absence of everything modern told him that wherever the storeroom had sent him, it had sent him backward, and the distance was not miles but years, and the number of years was large.

And then the dog barked.

The dog was lying on the far side of the fire, half-hidden behind the lean-to, and Colby hadn't seen it until it moved.

It was the ugliest dog Colby had ever seen. Not ugly in the way that bulldogs were ugly — ugly in a cultivated, bred-for-it way that people found charming. This dog was ugly in the way that life makes things ugly. It was medium-sized, maybe forty pounds, with a coat that was brown in some places and gray in others and missing entirely in patches along its ribs and haunches, as if the fur had decided that covering the whole body was more effort than it was worth. One ear stood up. The other flopped sideways. Its tail was crooked, bent at an angle halfway down, like it had been broken and healed wrong. Its eyes were brown and too large for its face, giving it the expression of a creature that had seen everything and was mildly disappointed by most of it.

The dog barked once — a single, declarative bark that was not aggressive and not friendly. It was informational. The bark said: there is a person here who was not here before. The bark was addressed to no one visible.

But someone answered.

"Founder, hush."

The voice came from behind the lean-to. It was deep, unhurried, with a roughness to it that sounded like gravel being poured slowly over wood. It was the voice of a man who talked to his dog the way some people talk to themselves — casually, without emphasis, because the conversation had been going on for years and neither party needed to raise their voice.

The dog — Founder — hushed. It sat back on its haunches and stared at Colby with its oversized brown eyes, and the stare was not hostile. It was evaluative. The dog was deciding something, and whatever it was deciding, it was taking its time.

A man came around the side of the lean-to.

He was carrying a wooden bucket in one hand and a skinned rabbit in the other, and he stopped when he saw Colby the way a person stops when they find something in their yard that wasn't there when they left — not alarmed, but curious, the pause of a man whose first instinct was to look before he reacted.

He was old. Not frail-old — weathered-old. The kind of old that comes from decades of living outside, where the sun and the wind and the cold write their history on a person's face in lines and creases and patches of skin that have been burned and healed and burned again so many times that the face becomes a map of everywhere the body has been. He was maybe five foot ten, lean, with arms that were ropy with muscle in the way that arms get when their owner has spent a lifetime swinging axes and hauling pelts and pulling himself over terrain that didn't have stairs. His beard was gray and full and reached his chest, and it was the kind of beard that had never been trimmed by anything sharper than a hunting knife, which meant it grew in every direction and looked like it had its own weather system.

He wore a buckskin shirt, dark with grease and use, and buckskin leggings and moccasins, and a hat made from something furry that Colby couldn't identify. Around his waist was a leather belt that held a knife, a pouch, and a coil of thin rope. Everything about him was brown and weathered and functional, as if the man and his clothes and his tools had all been made from the same material and assembled by the same hand.

He looked at Colby. He looked at Colby's sneakers. He looked at Colby's torn L&M polo shirt. He looked at Colby's jeans. He looked at Colby's face — the crooked nose that Arnold had broken and that had healed wrong, the dark circles under the eyes, the expression of a boy who was standing in a place that shouldn't exist and was doing his best not to fall apart.

The man set the bucket down. He set the rabbit down on a flat stone near the fire. He straightened up and put his hands on his hips and looked at Colby the way a person looks at a riddle — not confused, not suspicious, but interested in the way that a man who has lived alone in the woods for a long time is interested in anything that breaks the routine.

"Well," the man said to Colby. "You ain't no Indian. And you ain't no trapper. And you sure as hell ain't dressed for the woods." He tilted his head. "What are you?"

Colby opened his mouth. He closed it. He opened it again. The words that came out were not the words he'd planned, because he hadn't planned any words, because there were no words in the English language that adequately covered the situation of a fifteen-year-old stock boy standing in a frontier camp in what appeared to be the distant past, wearing a polo shirt with a grocery store logo on it.

"I don't know where I am," Colby said to the man.

The man nodded slowly, as if this were a perfectly reasonable thing for a boy in strange clothes to say in the middle of the Kentucky wilderness.

"Kentuckee. That's what the Shawnee call it. Dark and bloody ground. They ain't wrong." He spat into the fire. "Virginia claims it on paper. But Virginia ain't out here. Ain't no governor in these woods. Just trees and Indians and men like me who'd rather talk to a dog than a politician."

"Kentuckee," the man said to Colby. "Middle of it, more or less. East of the big river, south of the Ohio, north of nothing worth naming. Nearest settlement is maybe sixty miles that way." He pointed east. "But I wouldn't recommend walking it in those." He pointed at Colby's sneakers.

"Kentucky," Colby said. The word came out flat. He was from Idaho. Kentucky was two thousand miles away.

"Kentuckee," the man corrected. "That's what the Shawnee call it. Dark and bloody ground. They ain't wrong." He studied Colby's face. "You look like you ain't eaten in a day or two. Am I wrong about that?"

"No, sir," Colby said to the man. "You're not wrong."

The man picked up the rabbit and held it up by the back legs. It was skinned and cleaned, pink and glistening, ready for the spit.

"Sit down," the man said to Colby. The man set the bucket down. He hung the fresh rabbit on a hook near the pelts — that one was for later. Then he walked to the fire and checked the rabbit already on the spit.

"This one's about done. You'll eat and then you can tell me how a boy in peculiar clothes ended up in my camp without a weapon, a pack, or a lick of sense about where he is."

Colby sat. He sat because his legs were telling him to sit and because the man's voice, for all its roughness, had something underneath it that Colby recognized — not kindness exactly, but the absence of threat. The voice of a man who had no interest in hurting him. After fifteen years of calibrating his responses to the threat level in a room, Colby could read a voice the way a barometer reads pressure, and this man's voice read safe.

He sat on a log near the fire. The heat reached him immediately — the warmth of hardwood coals, steady and deep, nothing like the electric heater in the house on Spruce Street that Wanda kept on the lowest setting because electricity cost money. This heat was free. This heat came from the earth, from the trees, from the work of a man's hands, and it cost nothing and it asked nothing and it warmed Colby's wet clothes and his cold skin and something deeper than his skin that had been cold for a very long time.

The old man moved with the economy of a person who had performed every action in his day ten thousand times and had eliminated every wasted motion. No hurry. No hesitation. Just the smooth, practiced movements of a life lived in one place with one set of skills and no audience.

Founder got up from behind the lean-to. The dog walked around the fire, past the man, past the hanging pelts, and stopped in front of Colby. The oversized brown eyes looked up at him. The crooked tail moved — not a wag, not yet, but a twitch. A preliminary assessment.

Then Founder lay down next to Colby's leg. Not touching him. Just near him. Close enough that Colby could feel the warmth of the dog's body through the wet denim of his jeans.

The man watched this. His eyebrows rose a quarter of an inch — the only sign of surprise Colby had seen from him.

"Now that's something," the man said to Colby. "That dog don't lie down next to nobody. Took him three months before he'd sleep within ten feet of me, and I'm the one who feeds him."

"What's his name?" Colby asked the man.

"Founder. On account of he founded himself right here in my camp about two years back. Just showed up one morning. Mangy, skinny, half-starved, one ear chewed up, ribs showing through his hide like fence posts. I figured he'd eat and move on. He ate and stayed." The man looked at the dog with an expression that was trying to be indifferent and failing. "He ain't much to look at. But he's got sense. Better sense than most people I've met."

Colby looked down at Founder. The dog's eyes were closed. The crooked tail twitched once more and then was still. A stray that had wandered into a stranger's camp and decided to stay. A creature that had been damaged and starving and had found a place where the fire was warm and the man was decent and the food was enough. Colby understood that dog. He understood it in a way that went deeper than words, in the place where one broken thing recognizes another.

"I'm Colby," Colby said to the man. "Colby Utterback."

The man turned the rabbit on the spit. The fat dripped and the coals hissed and the smell of cooking meat filled the clearing.

"Skunk," the man said to Colby.

Colby waited for the rest of the name. It didn't come.

"Just Skunk?" Colby asked.

"Had another name once. Don't use it. Man named Harlan Prewitt gave me the name Skunk twenty-some years ago at a gathering on the Licking River, on account of I'd been sprayed three times in one season and he said I smelled like I'd lost a war with one." The man — Skunk — shrugged. "Name stuck. Names do that out here. You get called what you get called and after a while the name you were born with don't fit no more."

Colby almost smiled. He couldn't remember the last time he'd almost smiled. The motion felt foreign on his face, like a muscle being used after a long illness.

"How old are you, Colby Utterback?" Skunk asked.

"Fifteen," Colby said to Skunk.

"Fifteen." Skunk said the number the way a man says a number when he's measuring it against his own memory of what fifteen looked like. "You're big for fifteen. Thin, but big. Those shoulders didn't come from sitting still." He paused. "Who broke your nose?"

The question was direct. No cushion around it, no apology for asking. Skunk asked it the way he did everything — plainly, without performance, because a man who lived alone in the woods had no use for the social padding that people in towns wrapped around their words.

Colby's hand went to his nose. The crooked bridge. The bump where the bone had set wrong because Wanda couldn't afford a doctor and Arnold sure as hell wasn't going to pay for one.

"My stepfather," Colby said to Skunk.

Skunk's face didn't change. He didn't flinch, didn't tighten, didn't do any of the things that adults in Colby's experience did when he mentioned Arnold — the quick intake of breath, the careful expression, the performance of sympathy that was really the performance of discomfort. Skunk just looked at Colby and nodded once, slowly, the nod of a man who had lived long enough to know that the world contained men who hit children and that the fact of it was terrible and common and didn't require a reaction beyond acknowledgment.

"He still doing it?" Skunk asked Colby.

"No, sir. He's gone."

"Good. Because if he wasn't, I'd have a few things to say about it." Skunk turned the rabbit again. "Men who hit boys ain't men. They're dogs with hands. And I apologize to Founder for the comparison."

Founder's ear twitched. The dog did not appear offended.

The rabbit was done. Skunk pulled it off the spit, set it on the flat stone, and cut it with his skinning knife — quick, efficient, the blade separating meat from bone with the practiced ease of a man who had butchered more animals than Colby had stocked shelves. He put a piece on a wide leaf and handed it to Colby.

"Eat," Skunk said to Colby. "Then talk."

Colby ate. The rabbit was smoky and tender and tasted like nothing he'd ever had — not better than the cafeteria meatloaf or worse, just different, the taste of food that had been alive an hour ago and was cooked over a fire that someone had tended all night and served by a man who had killed it and cleaned it and offered it to a stranger without being asked. The taste of food that was given, not earned, not calculated, not measured against a budget. Just given.

He ate until the leaf was empty. Skunk gave him another piece without being asked. Colby ate that too. Founder watched the eating with the focused attention of a dog who had been hungry enough times to take the subject of food very seriously, and Skunk tossed the dog a piece of his own, and Founder caught it midair and swallowed it whole and looked at Skunk with the expression of a dog who believed that one piece was a strong opening offer but that negotiations should continue.

"Now," Skunk said to Colby. He sat down on a stump across the fire and put his hands on his knees and looked at Colby with the patient, unhurried attention of a man who had nowhere to be and nothing to do that was more important than listening. "Where did you come from, Colby Utterback, and how in the name of God's green earth did you end up in my woods wearing the strangest clothes I have ever seen on a human being?"

Colby told the truth.

Not all of it. Not the part about 2025 and Idaho and grocery stores and cars and airplanes and the internet. He knew without being told that none of that would make sense to this man, and that trying to explain it would make Colby sound insane, and that sounding insane to the only human being within sixty miles was not a survival strategy.

He told Skunk he'd been in a storeroom. That he'd walked through a gap in the back and ended up in the forest. That he didn't know how he'd gotten here or where here was or how to get back. He told it simply, without embellishment, because Colby Utterback had spent fifteen years stripping his words down to their smallest useful size, and the habit served him now.

Skunk listened. He didn't interrupt. He didn't ask clarifying questions. He sat on his stump and listened the way the forest listened — completely, without judgment, absorbing the words the way the ground absorbs rain.

When Colby finished, Skunk was quiet for a long time. The fire crackled. Founder shifted against Colby's leg. A hawk circled above the clearing, riding a thermal, patient and silent.

"I've been in these woods thirty years," Skunk said to Colby. "I've seen things that don't got names. Lights on the ridge that move like they're being carried but there ain't nobody carrying them. Sounds in the hollows that ain't animal and ain't human. Places in the deep woods where the air feels different — heavier, older, like the ground remembers something the rest of the world forgot." He looked at Colby. "I don't know where you came from. I don't know how you got here. But I know you ain't lying, because a liar would've come up with a better story."

Colby almost smiled again. This time the muscle moved a little farther. Not quite a smile, but the shadow of one, the outline.

"What year is it?" Colby asked Skunk.

Skunk scratched his beard. "Year of our Lord 1781, if I ain't lost count. Which I might have. Don't keep a calendar. The seasons tell me what I need to know, and the seasons don't need numbers."

1781. Colby's brain did the math one more time. 2025 minus 1781. Two hundred and forty-four years. He was sitting by a fire in a forest in Kentucky, two hundred and forty-four years before he was born, eating rabbit with a man named Skunk, while a one-eared dog slept against his leg.

The math didn't make sense. None of it made sense. But the fire was warm and the food was in his stomach and Founder was pressed against his leg and Skunk was looking at him with the steady, uncomplicated gaze of a man who didn't need things to make sense in order to deal with them, and Colby realized that for the first time in as long as he could remember, he was not afraid.

Not safe. He didn't know if he was safe. He didn't know if he could get home, or if home still existed, or if the storeroom and Corbin and Carl and Wanda and everything he'd left behind were still there on the other side of whatever he'd walked through. He didn't know anything.

But he was not afraid. And the absence of fear was so unfamiliar, so strange, so unlike anything he'd felt in the years since Arnold's hands had taught him that the world was a place where fear was the correct response to being alive, that Colby sat by the fire and felt the absence the way a person feels the absence of pain after carrying it for so long — like a sound that suddenly stops, and the silence that follows is so loud it has its own weight.

"You got people?" Skunk asked Colby. "Back where you came from?"

"My mother," Colby said to Skunk. "Five brothers and sisters. My little brother's sick."

He didn't know why he said the last part. Carl's asthma had nothing to do with anything. But the words came out because Carl was the first thing Colby thought about when he thought about home, and the inhaler was almost empty, and somewhere on the other side of two hundred and forty-four years a four-year-old boy was sleeping on a couch with his thumb in his mouth and his lungs were trying to kill him and Colby was not there to count his breaths.

Skunk looked at the fire. The flames had died to coals, orange and white, pulsing with heat. He reached over and put another piece of wood on, and the wood caught and the flames rose and the light in the clearing shifted from gold to amber.

"I had people once," Skunk said to Colby. "Wife. Boy. Cabin on the Clinch River in Virginia. Fever took them both in the same week. I was out trapping. Came home to a cold cabin and two graves that a neighbor had dug because nobody else was there to do it." He said it without emotion, the way a man says a thing that happened so long ago that the pain has become a scar and the scar has become just another part of his body. "That was twenty-six years ago. I came to Kentuckee because there was nothing left in Virginia worth staying for. Been here since."

Colby didn't say he was sorry. He knew from experience that sorry was a word people said when they didn't know what else to say, and Skunk didn't seem like a man who needed other people's words to manage his grief.

"You been alone since then?" Colby asked Skunk.

"Got Founder." Skunk looked at the dog. Founder was asleep, his ribs expanding and contracting with the slow, even rhythm of an animal that felt safe. "And I got the woods. And the woods don't talk back, which is a quality I have come to appreciate in my companions."

The clearing was quiet. The fire popped. The hawk was gone. The light through the canopy was shifting toward afternoon, the gold deepening, the shadows lengthening, and the forest around them was settling into the patient rhythm of a world that had been here long before either of them and would be here long after.

"You can stay," Skunk said to Colby. He said it the way he said everything — directly, without ceremony, as if the decision had been made before the words and the words were just a formality. "You can't go back the way you came, not tonight, not in those shoes, not without knowing the country. You stay, you eat, you sleep by the fire. In the morning we'll figure out what to do with you."

"Why?" Colby asked Skunk. The question came out before he could stop it — the question of a boy who had never been offered something without calculating what it would cost him.

Skunk looked at Colby. The gray eyes under the furry hat were clear and steady and held something that Colby had seen in very few adults in his life — the unperformative attention of a person who was looking at him and seeing him, not a problem to manage or a burden to carry or a mouth to feed, but a person. A boy. A human being who had shown up hungry and lost and needed help.

"Because you're here," Skunk said to Colby. "And I'm here. And that dog don't lie down next to just anybody, and I trust his judgment more than I trust mine." He stood. He stretched. His back popped audibly. "Besides, I been talking to myself and a one-eared dog for two years. A conversation with a whole human being might do me some good."

Colby looked at Founder. The dog was awake now, watching him with those oversized brown eyes, and the crooked tail moved again — not a twitch this time but a wag, slow and tentative, the wag of a dog who had decided something and was letting the boy know.

Colby reached down and put his hand on Founder's head. The fur was coarse and thin in places and warm from the fire. The dog leaned into his hand — pressed his skull against Colby's palm with a pressure that was gentle and deliberate, the pressure of an animal that had learned to trust slowly and was choosing to trust now.

A stray who had wandered into a camp and stayed. A boy who had walked through a gap and landed here. Two damaged things that had found each other in a clearing in a forest that existed in a year that hadn't existed for Colby until an hour ago.

Colby left his hand on the dog's head. The fire crackled. Skunk began cleaning the rabbit bones. The forest breathed around them, vast and old and indifferent to the impossibility of what had happened, because the forest had been here for ten thousand years and had seen stranger things than a boy from the future sitting by a fire with a trapper and a one-eared dog.

Colby didn't sleep that night. He lay by the fire under a deerskin that Skunk pulled from the lean-to and tossed to him without comment, and Founder curled against his side, and the warmth of the dog and the fire and the deerskin was more warmth than Colby had felt in years — not the physical kind, though that was part of it, but the other kind. The kind that comes from being in a place where nobody is going to hurt you and nobody expects anything from you and the only sound is the breathing of a dog who chose to lie next to you.

He stared at the sky. Through the gap in the canopy above the clearing, he could see stars — more stars than he had ever seen, more stars than he'd known existed, a sky so thick with light that it looked like the darkness had been painted on top of the brightness and was peeling off. No light pollution. No streetlights. No glow from a town. Just stars, and the stars were so many and so bright that they cast shadows, and Colby lay on his back in 1781 and looked at a sky that no living person in his world had ever seen, and the beauty of it was so sudden and so large that it hurt.

He thought about Carl. He thought about Wanda. He thought about Mary walking the kids to school and Shirley with her homework folder and Justin hiding under his blanket and Austin's arm hanging over the bunk.

He thought about the inhaler on the windowsill. Almost empty.

He thought about the table. The twenty. The shame in his mother's eyes.

And he lay under the stars in a world that was two hundred and forty-four years too early, with a dog against his ribs and a stranger's kindness in his stomach, and he did not cry, because Colby Utterback did not cry — Arnold had beaten that out of him before he was twelve. But something behind his eyes burned, the way a fire burns when it's banked and covered and not allowed to flame, and the burning was not sadness and was not fear.

It was the first faint recognition of something he had forgotten existed.

Hope.

Small. Uncertain. No bigger than the ember at the center of a dying fire. But there. Present. Warm.

Founder sighed against his ribs. The crooked tail twitched once. The stars turned slowly overhead, the way they had turned for ten thousand years, and Colby Utterback, fifteen years old, two hundred and forty-four years from home, closed his eyes and waited for sleep.

Chapter Four – Useful

Colby woke to the sound of an ax.

Not a sharp sound — not the crack of wood splitting. A duller rhythm, steady and patient, the sound of a blade biting into a log and being pulled free and biting again. He opened his eyes. The sky above the clearing was gray with early light, the kind of gray that comes just before sunrise when the world is awake but the sun hasn't committed yet. Founder was gone from his side. The deerskin was damp with dew.

Skunk was twenty yards away, at the edge of the clearing, chopping a fallen oak into sections. He swung the hatchet the way he did everything — without wasted motion, each stroke landing in the same groove as the last, the wood giving way in clean chunks that he kicked to the side with his moccasin. He'd been at it for a while. A pile of split wood sat near the fire pit, stacked in a way that said the man who stacked it had opinions about how firewood should be organized.

Founder was sitting near Skunk, watching the ax with his head tilted, one ear up, one flopped sideways, the expression of a dog who had seen this performance many times and still found it moderately interesting.

Colby sat up. His back ached from sleeping on the ground. His clothes were stiff with dried mud and dew and the general misery of fabric that had been wet and cold and slept in. His sneakers, sitting near the fire where he'd pulled them off the night before, looked like something a river had spit out.

Skunk stopped chopping. He looked at Colby across the clearing.

"You sleep like the dead," Skunk said to Colby. "I been making enough noise to wake the Shawnee nation and you didn't twitch."

"Sorry," Colby said to Skunk.

"Don't apologize. A boy who sleeps hard needed the sleep. Means your body trusts the ground it's on." Skunk set the hatchet down and walked to the fire. He stirred the coals with a stick and added two pieces from the pile and blew on them until they caught. "You hungry?"

"Yes, sir."

"Stop calling me sir. I ain't nobody's sir. Name's Skunk. You can use it."

Colby watched Skunk pull a blackened pot from behind the lean-to and set it on a flat stone near the fire. The pot held water. Skunk dropped something into it — dried leaves, dark and crumbled, from a pouch on his belt.

"That ain't real tea," Skunk said to Colby, as if he'd been accused. "Spicebush. Grows along the creek. Tastes like a tree that's trying to be polite. But it's hot and it'll wake your insides up."

He handed Colby a wooden cup when the water had steeped. The liquid was pale brown and smelled like bark and something faintly sweet. Colby drank it. It tasted exactly like a tree that was trying to be polite. He drank all of it.

Skunk ate leftover rabbit from the night before, cold, pulling strips of meat off the bone with his fingers. He gave Colby half without being asked. He gave Founder a piece. The three of them ate in the gray morning light, and the quiet between them was not the awkward quiet of strangers but the functional quiet of people who didn't need to talk to share a meal.

"Let me see those shoes," Skunk said to Colby after they'd eaten.

Colby handed him the sneakers. Skunk held them up. He turned them over. He bent the sole. He looked at the rubber and the synthetic mesh and the faded Nike swoosh with the expression of a man examining an object from another planet, which, in a sense, he was.

"What are these made of?" Skunk asked Colby.

"Rubber and fabric," Colby said to Skunk. The words sounded ridiculous. Rubber didn't exist here. Not the way

Colby knew it. Charles Goodyear wouldn't vulcanize rubber for another sixty years.

Skunk turned the sneaker over again. "It's light. I'll give it that. But the bottom's smooth as a creek stone, which means you'll slide off every rock and root in this forest. And the cloth is already tearing." He pointed to the rip from the branch that had caught Colby's sleeve yesterday, then at a hole forming near the toe. "Two weeks in these woods and these will be rags on your feet."

He tossed the sneakers back to Colby and walked to the lean-to. He rummaged behind the hanging pelts for a minute and came back with a pair of moccasins. They were worn — dark with use, the leather soft and creased, the soles thicker than the rest, stitched with sinew in a pattern that was rough but solid.

"These were mine before my feet decided to get wider," Skunk said to Colby. "Try them."

Colby pulled them on. They were too big — maybe half a size, enough to notice, not enough to matter. The leather was warm and the sole gripped the dirt when he stood, and the difference between the moccasins and the sneakers was the difference between wearing shoes and wearing the ground itself. He could feel every contour of the earth through the leather — rocks, roots, the soft give of leaves.

"They fit?" Skunk asked Colby.

"Little big."

"Stuff the toes with dried moss. They'll mold to your feet in a week. Leather does that. It learns the shape of whatever's inside it." Skunk looked at Colby's jeans and torn polo. "We'll have to do something about the rest of you too. Can't trap in those clothes. The deer'll hear you coming from a mile off, rustling like a bag of leaves."

"I don't know how to trap," Colby said to Skunk.

"I know you don't. That's why I'm going to teach you." Skunk said it the way he said everything — as a fact, not an offer. The decision had been made. Colby was here, Colby needed skills, and Skunk was the only teacher available. The math was simple and Skunk was a man who didn't waste time on math that was already done. "But first things first. You know how to build a fire?"

"With matches," Colby said to Skunk.

Skunk stared at him. "With what?"

Colby caught himself. Matches. Friction matches weren't invented until the 1820s. He was forty years too early for matches.

"Never mind," Colby said to Skunk. "No. I don't know how to build a fire."

Skunk nodded. His face showed nothing — no judgment, no disappointment. Just the practical acknowledgment of a man cataloging what needed to be taught.

"Water?" Skunk asked Colby. "You know how to find clean water?"

"From a creek, I guess," Colby said to Skunk.

"Which creek? The one upstream of where the elk are drinking, or the one downstream of where the elk are relieving themselves? There's a difference. The difference is three days of your guts turning inside out."

"Upstream," Colby said to Skunk.

"Good. You're not stupid. That helps." Skunk scratched his beard. "You know how to skin an animal?"

"No."

"Use a knife?"

"A kitchen knife. Not a —" Colby gestured at the skinning knife on Skunk's belt.

"Set a snare?"

"No."

"Read a track?"

"No."

"Shoot?"

"No."

Skunk looked at Colby for a long moment. Then he looked at Founder. Then he looked back at Colby.

"Boy," Skunk said to Colby, "you are the least prepared human being I have ever encountered in thirty years of living in these woods. And I once met a preacher from Philadelphia who tried to convert the Shawnee wearing silk stockings."

Colby felt his face go hot. The shame was automatic — the same shame he felt when Trent talked, the same shame he felt putting the twenty on the table, the shame of being insufficient. Of being less than. Of being the kid who couldn't do what needed doing.

But Skunk wasn't finished.

"However," Skunk said to Colby, and the word landed with the weight of a man who chose his words the way he chose his ax strokes — deliberately, one at a time, each one meant to land in a specific place. "You showed up in my camp half-starved and lost and wearing the strangest shoes God ever put on a foot, and you didn't cry. You didn't beg. You sat down and you ate and you told the truth and you slept by a fire next to a man you don't know in a place you can't explain. That takes guts. Guts I can work with. The rest is just skills, and skills can be taught."

The shame receded. Not all the way — shame never went all the way back, not for Colby, not after years of Arnold and Trent and the Goodwill jacket. But it receded enough for something else to come through. Something that felt like the faintest edge of standing up straight.

The first lesson was fire.

Skunk led Colby to a flat patch of ground near the lean-to and knelt down and opened his fire kit — a leather pouch that held a piece of flint, a curved piece of steel, and a bundle of charred cloth. He laid them out on the ground the way a surgeon lays out instruments, each one in its place, each one essential.

"Fire is the first thing," Skunk said to Colby. "Before food, before water, before shelter. A man with fire can survive almost anything. A man without fire is dead in three days in these mountains. Less in winter."

He showed Colby the strike — the steel held in the left hand, curved against the knuckles, the flint in the right, sharp edge angled down. A fast, glancing blow — steel against flint — and a spark jumped, bright orange, and landed on the charred cloth and caught. A tiny red eye of heat on the blackened fabric. Skunk picked up the cloth, placed it inside a bundle of dried grass, and blew — not hard, not panicked, a slow steady breath, feeding the ember the way you feed a newborn, carefully, patiently, with everything depending on the next breath and the next.

The grass caught. The ember became a flame. The flame became a fire.

"Your turn," Skunk said to Colby.

Colby's first attempt produced nothing. The steel glanced off the flint at the wrong angle and his knuckles hit the ground and the charred cloth sat there, cold and unimpressed.

"Angle's wrong," Skunk said to Colby. "You're chopping at it. Don't chop. Scrape. Like you're peeling the spark off the stone."

Second attempt. A spark flew, small, and missed the cloth.

"Closer," Skunk said to Colby. "Hold the cloth under the flint. The spark's got no sense of direction. You got to put the landing pad right where it falls."

Third attempt. Spark. Contact. A red pinpoint on the charred cloth. Colby picked it up, put it in the grass bundle, and blew. Too hard. The ember flared and died.

"You drowned it," Skunk said to Colby. "Fire's like a baby bird. You don't shove food down its throat. You offer it and let it eat."

Fourth attempt. Spark. Contact. Cloth into grass. Blow — gentle this time, slow, the breath coming from Colby's diaphragm the way Skunk had demonstrated, not from his cheeks. The ember glowed. The grass smoked. A thin line of flame licked up from the bundle, orange and alive, and Colby fed it a twig and the twig caught and he fed it another and another and the fire grew and the fire was his.

He looked up at Skunk. Skunk's face hadn't changed — the same weathered, bearded, unreadable expression that seemed to be the man's default setting. But his eyes had changed. The gray eyes under the furry hat held something that Colby had seen in very few adults in his life. Approval. Not the performed approval of a teacher handing back a graded paper. The real kind. The kind that comes from watching someone struggle and fail and try again and succeed, and knowing that the success was earned.

"Four tries," Skunk said to Colby. "That's better than most. Took me seven my first time, and I was twice your age and half again as stubborn."

The words landed in Colby's chest. Not like Lloyd's "Good job, son" — that landed like a stone in a well, echoing in the dark. This landed like a hand on his shoulder. Firm. Present. Real.

The rest of the morning was water.

Skunk took Colby to the creek — a clear, fast-running stream about fifty yards from camp, shallow enough to see the stones on the bottom, cold enough to make Colby's teeth ache when he cupped his hands and drank from it.

"You're drinking from the right spot," Skunk said to Colby, watching from the bank. "This stretch is above the camp. Water runs downhill. Anything you put in the water upstream comes downstream. So you drink upstream, you wash downstream, and you do your business further downstream than that. Get it backwards and you'll be the sickest boy in Kentuckee."

Colby nodded. The logic was obvious — the same logic he'd tried to explain to Austin last summer when Austin had wanted to splash in a puddle that was clearly runoff from the gas station parking lot. Water carried what was in it. The principle was the same in 2025 and 1781. Some things didn't change.

Skunk showed him where the spicebush grew — a shrub along the creek bank with smooth, dark leaves that smelled peppery when crushed. He showed him sassafras — the tree with three different leaf shapes, the roots that made tea. He showed him which mushrooms were food and which were death, and the difference between the two was sometimes nothing more than the color of the gills, and Skunk's voice got harder when he talked about the death ones.

"This one will kill you," Skunk said to Colby, pointing at a white mushroom with a smooth cap. "And it'll take three days to do it, and the three days will be the worst of your life.

Learn it. Don't eat anything you can't name. If you can't name it, bring it to me. If I can't name it, we don't eat it. Agreed?"

"Agreed," Colby said to Skunk.

They worked through the afternoon.

Skunk showed Colby how to carry water in the wooden bucket without slopping it over the sides — a matter of stride length and rhythm, the bucket held low against the hip, the body moving around the water instead of the water moving with the body. He showed him how to gut the second rabbit — the one Skunk had hung on the hook that morning. The knife went in below the ribs and opened the belly in a single clean line, and the insides came out in a slick, hot mass that Founder appeared from nowhere to investigate with the detailed attention of a food critic reviewing a new restaurant.

Colby's stomach turned the first time. Not from disgust — he had seen worse things than animal guts in his fifteen years. It turned from the strangeness of it, the intimacy of reaching inside a dead animal and pulling out the machinery that had kept it alive. But the turning passed, and Skunk showed him how to separate the organs — heart, liver, kidneys to keep, intestines and stomach to discard — and Colby did it, and his hands were steady, and Skunk watched without comment, which Colby was beginning to understand was the highest form of praise the man offered.

He scraped the pelt. Skunk gave him a flat stone with a sharp edge and showed him how to stretch the hide on a frame and scrape the fat and membrane from the underside in long, even strokes, working from the center outward, the way you'd sand a piece of wood. The work was hard — the stone was heavy, the strokes had to be firm enough to clean the hide but gentle enough not to tear it, and Colby's arms burned after twenty minutes.

He didn't stop. He didn't ask to stop. He scraped until the hide was clean, because Colby Utterback had spent seven months stacking shelves and unloading trucks and sweeping floors at L&M Food Center, and before that he had spent six years absorbing Arnold's fists and his mother's exhaustion and his family's poverty without complaint, and the one thing that all of it had given him — the only gift that a hard life gives — was the ability to work through pain without stopping.

Skunk saw it. He didn't say anything. But he saw it — the way the boy's jaw set when his arms started shaking, the way his hands kept moving after his muscles said stop, the way he finished the job and set the stone down and didn't rub his arms or flex his fingers or do any of the things that a person does when they want someone to notice how hard they've worked. Colby didn't want anyone to notice. Colby just worked, because work was the one language he spoke fluently, and in this world, for the first time, the language was useful.

"You've done this before," Skunk said to Colby. Not the scraping — they both knew Colby had never scraped a hide. The working. The keeping-on when the keeping-on got hard. Skunk recognized it because he'd spent thirty years in a profession that was nothing but keeping-on.

"I've had jobs," Colby said to Skunk.

"That ain't what I mean." Skunk looked at Colby the way he'd looked at him the night before, when Colby had mentioned his stepfather — the steady, unemotional gaze of a man reading a story written on another person's body. The crooked nose. The thin frame that was strong underneath the thinness. The shoulders that pulled in and then caught themselves and straightened, the habit of a boy who had been made small and was trying to remember how to be full-sized. "You've done hard things. Real hard things. And you didn't quit."

Colby didn't answer. He didn't know how to answer, because nobody had ever said that to him before. Teachers had said he was smart. Lloyd had said "Good job, son." Uncle James had told the judge that Colby was a good kid. But nobody had ever looked at the work he'd done just to survive his own life and called it what it was.

"That's the most important skill there is," Skunk said to Colby. "Everything else I can teach you. But that — the not-quitting — that's yours. You brought that with you."

By evening, Colby had built two fires, carried four buckets of water, gutted a rabbit, scraped a hide, and learned the names of eleven plants.

His arms shook when he lifted the cup of spicebush tea that Skunk handed him. His back ached from bending over the hide frame. His hands were raw from the flint and the scraping stone and the bark of the firewood he'd split with Skunk's hatchet, badly at first — the wood jumping sideways, the blade glancing — and then better, the rhythm finding itself the way rhythms do when the body is allowed to learn without the mind getting in the way.

He sat by the fire. Founder lay beside him — not near him anymore, but beside him, the dog's body pressed against Colby's leg, the crooked tail resting across Colby's ankle. The distance between near and beside was small in feet and enormous in meaning, and Colby felt it the way he felt the moccasins molding to his feet — a thing that was learning his shape.

Skunk sat across the fire. He was carving something from a piece of hickory — a handle, maybe, or a peg. The knife moved in slow, precise curls, the shavings falling around his moccasins like pale ribbons. The fire crackled between them, and the clearing was quiet except for the fire and the creek and the sound of the knife against wood.

"Skunk," Colby said.

"Hm."

"How do I get back?"

Skunk didn't look up from his carving. The knife kept moving. Curl, curl, curl. The shavings fell.

"I don't know," Skunk said to Colby. "I don't know how you got here, so I sure don't know how you get back. I expect the getting-back works the same as the getting-here — it'll happen when it happens, and pushing on it won't help."

"What if it doesn't happen?" Colby asked Skunk.

Skunk looked up. The firelight caught his face — the lines, the gray beard, the eyes that had seen thirty years of wilderness and two graves on the Clinch River and the inside of a loneliness that most people couldn't survive.

"Then you learn to live here," Skunk said to Colby. "And I teach you how. And that dog keeps lying next to you every night. And the world you came from becomes a story you carry inside you, the way I carry Virginia."

He went back to his carving. The knife moved. The shavings fell. Founder's ribs expanded and contracted against Colby's leg, slow and steady.

"But I'll tell you something, Colby Utterback," Skunk said without looking up. "You walked through something to get here. Whatever it was, it brought you to my camp. Not to the river, not to the settlements, not to the Shawnee. To my camp. I been here two years and nobody has found this place. Not a soul. And then you walk out of the trees in shoes made of nothing I've ever seen and a shirt with writing on it, and my dog — who don't trust nobody — lies down at your feet." He looked at Colby. "That ain't an accident. I don't know what it is, but it ain't an accident."

Colby looked at Founder. The dog's eyes were closed. The crooked tail lay across his ankle like a comma at the end of a sentence that wasn't finished yet.

He didn't know what it was either. He didn't know why the storeroom had opened into a forest or why the forest had led to this camp or why this dog had chosen him. He didn't know if he'd get home or when or how.

But he knew one thing that he hadn't known yesterday.

He was useful. Today, for the first time in his life, his hands had done things that mattered — not stacking shelves for $8.50 an hour, not putting twenties on a table that swallowed them, but real things. Fire. Water. Food. The fundamental acts of staying alive, performed with his own hands, and the man who'd watched him do it had looked at him and seen someone worth teaching.

That was new. That was so new it didn't have a place in Colby's chest yet. It sat on the surface, like the moccasins that hadn't molded to his feet yet, present but not quite his.

It would be, though. Given time. Leather learns the shape of whatever's inside it.

Colby drank his tea. The fire burned. Founder breathed against his leg. And somewhere on the other side of two hundred and forty-four years, the storeroom at L&M Food Center sat empty and dark, and the gap at the back of the shelves was just a gap, and the concrete floor was just concrete, and the world that Colby had left didn't know he was gone.

Chapter Five - Earning It

The days found a rhythm.

Colby didn't notice it happening. It was like the moccasins — one morning they were stiff and too big and foreign on his feet, and then a week passed and they weren't. The leather had learned his shape. The days had learned his shape too, or he had learned theirs, and the difference didn't matter because the result was the same: he woke before dawn, he built the fire, he boiled the spicebush tea, and by the time Skunk came back from checking the trap line, the camp was warm and the water was hot and the day had a direction.

Two weeks. That's how long it took for Colby Utterback to stop feeling like a guest in Skunk's camp and start feeling like a part of it.

The work helped. There was always work. In Idaho, work had been a four-hour shift at L&M — stacking shelves, sweeping floors, tasks that started and stopped with a clock. Here, work didn't have a clock. It had the sun. You started when the light was enough to see by and you stopped when it wasn't, and between those two points the day was full of things that needed doing, and every one of them kept you alive.

Colby chopped wood. He hauled water. He tended the fire — not just building it but keeping it, banking the coals at night so the morning fire could be coaxed back without wasting flint and steel. He learned that a good fire was not a big fire but a steady one, and that the difference between the two was the difference between showing off and surviving, and Skunk had no patience for showing off.

He learned the trap line. Skunk ran twelve traps in a circuit that took half a day to walk — steel-jawed traps for beaver, deadfalls for rabbit and marten, snares made of twisted rawhide for anything fast and stupid enough to run through a gap between two trees without looking up. The traps were set along creek beds and game trails and the narrow corridors between ridges where animals traveled the same paths their grandparents had traveled, because animals were creatures of habit, and habit was what made them catchable.

Skunk showed Colby how to read the signs — the chewed bark that meant beaver, the droppings that meant deer, the scratched earth that meant turkey. He showed him how to set a snare: the loop sized for the animal's head, the anchor tied to a branch heavy enough to hold but flexible enough to give, the trigger balanced so delicately that a nudge would spring it.

"A snare ain't a fight," Skunk said to Colby as they crouched by a game trail on the fifth morning. "It's an invitation. You're asking the animal to walk through a door. If the door looks wrong — wrong smell, wrong height, wrong feel — the animal walks around it. You got to think like the thing you're trying to catch. Where does it want to go? What does it expect to see? Put the snare where the animal already wants to be, and let the animal do the rest."

Colby set his first snare that morning. Skunk watched without helping — arms crossed, leaning against a hickory, Founder sitting at his feet with the evaluative expression of a supervisor overseeing a new hire. Colby tied the loop, sized it, hung it at the height Skunk had shown him, anchored the line, balanced the trigger. His fingers were clumsy. The rawhide was stiff and didn't want to cooperate. The trigger fell twice before he got it balanced.

"Leave it," Skunk said to Colby when it was done. "We'll check it tomorrow. Don't touch it again. Your smell is on it now, and the less of your smell the better. The animal don't know you. You're a stranger in its woods. Give it a day to forget you were here."

The next morning, the snare held a rabbit.

Colby saw it from twenty yards away — the brown shape hanging from the trigger branch, motionless, the loop tight around the neck. The rabbit was dead. It had been dead for hours, the body stiff, the eyes glazed, the fur damp with dew. Colby stood in front of it and felt something he had not expected to feel.

Not guilt. He had thought he would feel guilt — the guilt of killing a living thing, even indirectly, even through a mechanism of rope and wood that had done the actual work while Colby slept. But the guilt didn't come. What came instead was something quieter and more complicated: the recognition that this animal was dead because of something Colby had built with his own hands, and the death meant food, and food meant survival, and survival was not a thing that was given to you. It was a thing you went out and earned.

He had never earned anything before. Not really. The $8.50 an hour at L&M was earned in the technical sense — labor exchanged for money — but it was someone else's store and someone else's shelves and someone else's system, and Colby was a part in a machine that would run without him. This was different. This rabbit was in the snare because Colby had set the snare, and nobody else had helped, and nobody else would eat it if he didn't bring it back.

He carried the rabbit to camp by its back legs, the way Skunk carried them. Founder trotted beside him, nose working, eyes locked on the rabbit with the focused intensity of a dog for whom the distinction between food and not-food was the most important distinction in the world.

Skunk was at the fire. He looked up. He saw the rabbit. He didn't smile — Skunk's face didn't do things as obvious as smiling — but something shifted behind his eyes, a movement like sunlight passing behind a cloud, there and gone.

"Your first," Skunk said to Colby.

"My first," Colby said to Skunk.

"Gut it. Skin it. Cook it. That's yours start to finish."

Colby gutted it. He skinned it — clumsily, nicking the hide in two places where the knife went too deep, losing a patch of fur near the haunch that Skunk would have saved. He spitted it and set it over the coals and turned it when the fat started dripping and pulled it off when the meat was brown and the smell of it filled the clearing with the smell of something he had made happen.

He ate it sitting on the log by the fire. Founder got the scraps. Skunk ate his own breakfast — cold venison from the day before — and watched Colby eat the way a man watches a thing he's been building finally do what it was built to do.

"How's it taste?" Skunk asked Colby.

Colby chewed. The rabbit was smoky and a little tough and he'd cooked it too long on one side and not long enough on the other. It was not as good as the rabbit Skunk had made him the first night. It was the best thing he had ever eaten.

"Like mine," Colby said to Skunk.

Skunk's beard moved. It was the closest thing to a smile Colby had seen from the man — a rearrangement of the gray hairs around his mouth that lasted about half a second and then was gone, absorbed back into the weathered, unreadable landscape of his face.

"It'll get better," Skunk said to Colby. "The cooking and the catching. Everything gets better when you keep doing it. That's the only secret there is."

His clothes died on the ninth day.

The L&M polo shirt went first. The branch tear from his walk through the forest had widened into a rip that ran from the sleeve to the hem, and the fabric — thin polyester blend, designed for a climate-controlled grocery store, not a wilderness — had given up the way things give up when they're asked to do something they were never made for. Colby pulled it on one morning and the collar ripped clean away from the shoulder, and he stood in the clearing holding the two pieces of what used to be his work uniform and realized he was looking at the last physical piece of L&M Food Center, and it was dead.

The jeans lasted two days longer. The knees went, then the seat, then the seam along the left thigh where a branch had been working at it for a week. By the eleventh day Colby was wearing the bottom half of his jeans as shorts and the top half of nothing, and Skunk looked at him across the fire and shook his head.

"You look like something the creek spit out," Skunk said to Colby. "Which is an improvement over the peculiar clothes, but we can do better."

Skunk had two deer hides — scraped, smoked, and softened into the pale golden leather that frontier people called buckskin. He laid them out on the ground and studied Colby's frame the way a tailor studies a customer, except this tailor was barefoot and smelled like wood smoke and his measuring tool was his own hands held at arm's length.

"Stand there," Skunk said to Colby. "Arms out."

Colby stood. Skunk circled him once, grunting at intervals, a sound that might have meant satisfaction or might have meant the opposite. Then he sat down with his skinning knife and started cutting.

The shirt took a day. It was simple — two panels, front and back, stitched at the shoulders and sides with sinew, open at the neck, the sleeves loose enough to move in. Skunk cut it long, past Colby's hips, and left the bottom edge unfinished because finishing was for people who cared about appearances and Skunk cared about function.

The leggings took another day. They tied at the waist with a rawhide cord and hung loose around the legs, and when Colby put them on and stood in the clearing in his buckskins and his moccasins, he looked down at himself and did not recognize what he saw.

Not the clothes. The clothes were strange but they fit, and the leather was warm and the weight of it on his shoulders felt different from any fabric he'd ever worn — heavier, more present, as if the clothes were aware of his body the way his body was aware of them. What Colby didn't recognize was the boy wearing the clothes. The boy who had walked into this clearing two weeks ago in a torn polo and falling-apart sneakers was gone. The boy standing here now had calluses on his hands and soot under his fingernails and a knife on his belt that Skunk had given him without ceremony — a spare, short-bladed, with a handle worn smooth by years of use — and the boy's shoulders were not pulled in.

They were back. Not all the way. But back — wider, higher, occupying space that Colby had surrendered years ago to Arnold's fists and Trent's words. The shoulders didn't know yet that they were allowed to stay out. They were testing it, the way a dog tests a new room — carefully, ready to retreat.

But they were out.

Skunk looked at Colby in the buckskins. He nodded once.

"Now you look like you belong somewhere," Skunk said to Colby.

Colby didn't answer. He was afraid that if he opened his mouth, something would come out that he couldn't put back — not tears, because Colby didn't cry, but the thing that lived behind the tears, the pressure that built when something true was said to a person who wasn't used to hearing true things.

Now you look like you belong somewhere.

Nobody had ever said that to him. Not in those words. Not in any words. Colby Utterback had spent fifteen years looking like he belonged nowhere — not in Arnold's house, not in Corbin High, not at the table in the cafeteria, not even in his own skin. And now a man in a furry hat who smelled like wood smoke and talked to a one-eared dog had looked at him in a pair of buckskins and said the thing that Colby didn't know he'd been waiting his whole life to hear.

The nights were different from the days.

During the day, Colby was busy. The work filled his hands and his mind and left no room for the thoughts that lived in the spaces between tasks. But at night, when the fire was banked and Skunk was snoring in the lean-to and Founder was pressed against Colby's ribs under the deerskin, the thoughts came.

Carl was the first thought. Always Carl. The small body on the couch, the blanket that used to be blue, the thumb that was a diagnostic tool and a comfort and the only thing a four-year-old boy had that was entirely his own. Was the inhaler empty by now? Had Wanda found the money for a new one? Was someone listening for the wheezing at night, or was Carl lying on that couch in the dark with his lungs closing and nobody there to press the inhaler to his lips and say

Breathe in when I press it, big breath, like blowing up a balloon but backwards?

Then Wanda. The spatula hitting the pan. The coffee going cold. Was the twenty on the table? It couldn't be. Colby wasn't there to put it there.

He thought about the rest of them — not the details, because the details were always the same and always would be. Just the weight of five people who needed him and didn't know where he was.

Colby lay under the stars and the guilt pressed on his chest like a stone. He was here. They were there. He was eating rabbit and learning to trap and wearing buckskins by a fire with a man who said he belonged somewhere, and his family was in a three-bedroom rental on the wrong side of the tracks in Corbin, Idaho, counting on money he wasn't sending and care he wasn't giving and a presence he couldn't provide.

The guilt said: you should be there. The guilt said: they need you. The guilt said: what kind of person finds a place where he's happy and stays while his family suffers?

But Colby couldn't go back. Not tonight. Not tomorrow. He didn't know how he'd gotten here and he didn't know how to get back, and pushing on it, as Skunk had said, wouldn't help. The portal had brought him here and the portal would take him home when the portal was ready, and until then Colby was stuck in 1781 with a trapper and a dog and a sky full of stars that nobody in his world had ever seen.

So he lay there. And he did what he always did with things he couldn't fix. He carried them. Quietly. Without complaint. The way he carried the twenty to the table and the weight through the school doors and the knowledge that the door at the end of the hallway was always there.

Except the door was farther away now. He noticed it the way you notice a sound that has stopped — not by hearing the silence but by remembering the noise. The thought —

what if I wasn't here

— had not come since he'd arrived in Kentucky. Not once. The door was still there, somewhere, in the back of the hallway where it had always been. But the hallway was longer now. The hallway had a fire in it, and a dog, and a man who said he had guts, and the door was farther away than it had been in a long time.

That was something. It wasn't enough — it wasn't home, it wasn't Carl's breathing, it wasn't the twenty on the table. But it was something.

Founder shifted against his ribs. The crooked tail settled across Colby's wrist. The dog sighed — the deep, total sigh of an animal that had found its place and was done looking.

Colby put his hand on Founder's side and felt the ribs expand and contract. He counted the breaths the way he counted Carl's breaths — ten, twenty, all steady. A habit built for one purpose, used for another. A boy who counted his brother's breathing was now counting his dog's breathing, and the counting meant the same thing it had always meant.

Still here. Still breathing. Still mine to watch over.

On the fourteenth morning, Skunk did something unexpected.

He laughed.

They were at the creek, washing. Colby had been scrubbing his face with the cold water, and when he stood up Founder was standing behind him with Colby's moccasin in his mouth — the left one, stolen from the rock where Colby had set it, held gently between the dog's teeth with the expression of an animal who knew exactly what he'd done and was prepared to negotiate.

"Founder," Colby said to the dog. "Give it back."

Founder's crooked tail wagged. The moccasin stayed in his mouth. The oversized brown eyes communicated a clear and specific message: make me.

Colby stepped toward the dog. Founder stepped backward. Colby stepped again. Founder turned and trotted three paces and stopped and looked over his shoulder, the moccasin dangling from his jaws like a trophy.

"Founder. Drop it."

The tail wagged harder. The dog was enjoying this. The dog was, for the first time since Colby had met him, playing.

Colby lunged. Founder bolted. The dog ran a wide circle around the clearing with the moccasin in his mouth, ears back, legs churning, the crooked tail streaming behind him like a broken flag, and the run was not the run of a dog being chased but the run of a dog who had discovered joy and was testing it at full speed.

And then the sound came from behind Colby — a sound he hadn't heard from the man in two weeks of living in his camp. It was deep and rough and completely unrehearsed, a sound that came from somewhere below Skunk's beard and erupted through his chest like something that had been locked in a box and had finally found the lid open.

Skunk was laughing.

Not chuckling. Not grinning. Laughing — the full, uncontrolled laugh of a man who had spent two years talking to a dog and had forgotten what it felt like to find something genuinely funny, and the sight of his dog running circles around a barefoot boy in buckskins had reminded him.

Colby looked at Skunk. Skunk was bent at the waist, one hand on his knee, the other waving at Founder as if the dog needed encouragement. His face was transformed — the lines rearranged, the gray eyes creased, the mouth open behind the beard in a way that showed teeth that were mostly still there and a tongue that was not used to the shape of laughter.

And Colby laughed.

He didn't decide to. The laugh came out of him the way Skunk's had — involuntary, unstoppable, a sound from a place so deep inside him that he hadn't known the place existed. It was not a loud laugh. It was not a long laugh. It was a short, startled burst of sound that felt foreign in his mouth, like speaking a language he'd learned as a child and forgotten.

But it was real. It was the first real laugh he'd laughed in so long that the muscles in his face didn't know what to do with it, and his eyes burned, and for one terrible, wonderful second he thought the laugh might turn into something else — into the thing that Arnold had beaten out of him, the thing he hadn't done since he was twelve.

It didn't. The laugh stayed a laugh. And Founder came trotting back with the moccasin and dropped it at Colby's feet and sat down and looked up at him with the expression of a dog who had accomplished something important and expected to be recognized for it.

Colby picked up the moccasin. It was wet with dog spit. He didn't care.

Skunk straightened up. He wiped his eyes with the back of his hand. He looked at Colby, and the look was different from any look the man had given him before — not the evaluative look, not the practical look, not the reading-the-story-on-your-body look. This look was simpler. Warmer.

"That dog," Skunk said to Colby, shaking his head. "That worthless, thieving, one-eared dog."

But the way he said it was the way a man says the name of something he loves.

Colby put the moccasin on. Wet and all. He looked at Skunk. He looked at Founder. He looked at the clearing — the fire, the lean-to, the pelts on the rack, the creek where the water caught the morning light and threw it back in pieces.

Two weeks. He had been here two weeks. He was a long way from home, and home was a long way from being fixed, and the guilt was still there and the worry was still there and Carl was still breathing on a couch in a house he couldn't reach.

But he had laughed. And somewhere in the laughing, in the involuntary, unstoppable eruption of a sound he'd forgotten he could make, something had shifted. Not broken. Not healed. Shifted — the way a bone shifts when it's being set, painful and necessary, the body moving toward the position it was always supposed to be in.

Colby Utterback was finding his place.

Chapter Six - The Track

A month in, Skunk handed Colby the rifle.

Not to shoot. To hold. The flintlock was longer than Colby expected and heavier than it looked, the dark wood stock smooth from decades of handling, the metal barrel cold against his palm. It smelled like oil and gunpowder and something older — the accumulated scent of a thousand fires and a hundred kills and the hands of a man who had carried it through thirty years of wilderness.

"That rifle has a name," Skunk said to Colby. "Judith. Named her after my mother, who was also long and loud and didn't suffer fools."

Colby held Judith. The weight settled into his arms the way weight always settled into his arms — naturally, without complaint, his body accepting one more thing to carry because his body had been carrying things since before it was ready.

Skunk showed him how to load. Powder first — measured from a horn, poured down the barrel, a precise amount that Skunk could gauge by feel but that Colby had to measure twice and second-guess three times. Then the patch — a small square of greased cloth that held the ball snug in the barrel. Then the ball itself — lead, round, heavy in Colby's fingers, warm from his pocket. Ram it home with the rod. Prime the pan. Pull the hammer to full cock.

"The whole thing takes thirty seconds if you're practiced," Skunk said to Colby. "A minute if you're not. Which means you get one shot. Miss, and the deer is gone before you can reload. Miss in a fight, and it's worse than gone."

"I'm not planning on fighting anybody," Colby said to Skunk.

"Nobody plans on it. That's why they call it a fight and not an appointment."

"Colby practiced the loading sequence for three days before Skunk let him fire. Skunk had him run through the motions with an empty rifle — measure the powder, seat the patch and ball at the muzzle, ram it home, prime the pan. Over and over, hands learning the steps, until his fingers moved through the sequence without his brain telling them to. Then Skunk let him load for real

The first shot was loud enough to scare a flock of crows out of the canopy and send Founder scrambling behind the lean-to with his crooked tail between his legs. The ball hit a tree trunk twenty feet left of the mark Skunk had carved. Colby's shoulder ached from the kick.

"You flinched," Skunk said to Colby. "Everybody flinches the first time. The gun's loud and the kick's hard and your body thinks it's being attacked. It ain't. It's a tool. Treat it like one."

By the fifth shot, Colby could hit the tree. By the tenth, he could hit the mark. Not every time. But enough that Skunk stopped watching with his arms crossed and started watching with his hands on his hips, which Colby had learned was the difference between evaluating and approving.

The tracking lesson came on a morning in late November.

The first frost had come and gone, and the forest had changed. The canopy was thinner — the oaks and hickories had dropped their leaves, and the light that reached the ground was brighter and colder, the light of a world that was stripping itself down to its bones for winter. The air smelled like frozen earth and wood smoke. Colby could see his breath.

Skunk woke him early. Earlier than usual — the sky was still black, the stars still showing through the bare branches overhead.

"Get up," Skunk said to Colby. "Bring Judith. We're hunting today."

They left camp before dawn. Founder came, moving through the undergrowth in the silent, low-bellied trot that was his hunting walk — different from his camp walk, different from his playing walk, a version of the dog that was older and more serious than the one who stole moccasins. In the woods, Founder was a different animal. His nose worked constantly, sweeping the air, reading messages that Colby couldn't see or smell or understand.

Skunk walked ahead. He moved through the forest the way water moves through rock — finding the gaps, following the path of least resistance, his moccasins landing on the ground without sound. Colby followed and tried to be as quiet and was not, his feet finding every dry stick and dead leaf that Skunk's feet had avoided, and behind him Founder moved more quietly than both of them combined, which was embarrassing.

After an hour, Skunk stopped. He knelt. He pointed at the ground.

"What do you see?" Skunk asked Colby.

Colby looked. The ground was soft from the frost melt — dark earth, scattered leaves, a patch of mud near a seep. In the mud was a shape. Two shapes. Indentations in the earth, roughly oval, with pointed tips.

"Tracks," Colby said to Skunk.

"What kind?"

Colby looked closer. The tracks were larger than rabbit, smaller than the bear prints Skunk had shown him near the creek last week. They were split down the middle — two halves of an oval, like a heart pressed into the mud.

"Deer," Colby said to Skunk.

"How many?"

Colby studied the ground. This was where his brain did something useful. The brain that calculated rent and counted heads and measured inhaler puffs and tracked Trent's movements through the hallways of Corbin High — that brain was built for patterns. It saw what was there and what wasn't there and the relationship between the two, and it did it automatically, the way Skunk's hands automatically loaded a rifle.

Two sets of tracks. One larger, the hooves spread wider, the impression deeper in the mud. One smaller, the stride shorter, the prints shallower.

"Two," Colby said to Skunk. "A big one and a small one. Doe and a fawn, maybe."

Skunk looked at him. The gray eyes were sharp under the furry hat.

"Why not a buck?" Skunk asked Colby.

"No drag marks," Colby said to Skunk. He didn't know where the answer came from. He'd never tracked an animal in his life. But he'd seen the buck tracks Skunk had pointed out last week, and those tracks had small lines behind them where the buck's hooves dragged in the soft ground because bucks walked heavier than does, especially in fall when they were thick-necked and heavy from the rut. These tracks were clean. No drag. Light on the ground.

Skunk's eyebrows rose. Just a fraction. The equivalent of a standing ovation from a man who expressed emotion the way a telegraph expressed poetry — in short, coded bursts that required interpretation.

"You got eyes," Skunk said to Colby. "Real eyes. The kind that see what's there instead of what you want to be there. Most people can't do that. They see what they expect and miss everything else."

Colby felt the words land in the place where Skunk's words always landed — not the well where Lloyd's "son" echoed, but the newer place, the one that was being built out of fire-starting and hide-scraping and rabbit-catching, the place where competence lived. The place that said: you can do this.

They followed the tracks.

Tracking was reading.

Colby understood this within the first hour, and once he understood it, the forest changed. It went from a place of trees and dirt and random shapes to a place of information — a page covered in writing that he was learning to decode. Every bent branch was a sentence. Every scuffed patch of ground was a word. The droppings were timestamps. The browsed vegetation — the stripped bark, the chewed twigs, the mushrooms bitten at a specific height — told him what the animal was eating and how long ago it had stopped to eat.

Skunk walked beside him now, not ahead. The shift was deliberate. Skunk was letting Colby lead.

"She went left here," Colby said to Skunk, pointing at a disturbed patch of leaves where the doe had veered off the game trail toward a thicket of mountain laurel. "The fawn followed. The tracks overlap."

"How long ago?" Skunk asked Colby.

Colby knelt. The tracks were sharp-edged, the walls of the impressions still holding their shape. No leaves had fallen into them. No dew had softened the edges.

"This morning," Colby said to Skunk. "Early. Before the frost melted. The edges are still hard."

Skunk nodded. He said nothing. The nothing was loud.

Founder was ahead of them both, nose down, tail level, moving through the laurel in a low crouch that said the dog knew exactly where the deer was and was waiting for the humans to catch up. The dog had been doing this longer than Colby and with better equipment, and there were moments when Colby suspected that Founder considered the entire tracking lesson a waste of time that could have been avoided if the humans had simply followed the dog in the first place.

They found the doe an hour later.

She was in a clearing — a small one, maybe thirty feet across, where a fallen tree had opened a gap in the canopy and the sunlight poured through in a column of gold. She was browsing on the low branches of a young maple, her head down, her ears rotating like radar dishes, the fawn at her side. The fawn was small — born in the spring, still spotted along the flanks, its legs too long for its body in the way that young things are always slightly wrong in their proportions.

Colby's heart was beating hard. Skunk was behind him, motionless, invisible against a hemlock trunk. Founder was flat on his belly, twenty feet to the left, still as stone.

Skunk had told Colby the rule. You don't shoot the doe when she's with a fawn. The fawn can't survive alone. You take the doe, you kill the fawn too — slow, over days, from starvation or predators. That's not hunting. That's waste.

So they watched. The doe lifted her head. She chewed. Her dark eyes scanned the tree line, passed over the spot where Colby crouched, and moved on. She hadn't seen him. The buckskins blended with the bark and the dead leaves, and Colby was downwind, and the doe's nose — which was better than Founder's and a thousand times better than Colby's — couldn't find him.

He stayed still for twenty minutes. His legs cramped. His fingers were numb around Judith's stock. The doe ate and moved and ate again, and the fawn pressed against her side, and the clearing was quiet except for the sound of teeth on bark and the distant call of a jay.

Then the doe raised her head sharply. Her ears locked forward. Her body went rigid — the posture of an animal that had detected something and was deciding between standing and running. Colby froze. He didn't breathe. The doe stared in his direction for five eternal seconds.

Then she turned and walked into the trees, the fawn following, their white tails flashing once and then gone, and the clearing was empty and the column of gold light fell on nothing.

Colby exhaled. His legs shook when he stood. Skunk appeared beside him, materializing from behind the hemlock as if he'd grown there.

"You didn't shoot," Skunk said to Colby.

"The fawn," Colby said to Skunk.

Skunk looked at Colby the way he looked at him when the boy did something right — not the eyebrow raise, not the beard twitch, but the deeper thing, the look that came from behind the gray eyes and said

I see you.

"There'll be a buck," Skunk said to Colby. "Rut's ending. The bucks are alone now, moving ridge to ridge. We'll find one tomorrow or the day after. And when we do, you'll take the shot."

He paused.

"But today you did the harder thing. Any fool can pull a trigger. It takes something else to not pull it when you've got the reason not to."

They found the buck two days later.

He was alone, the way Skunk had predicted — a six-pointer, thick through the shoulders, moving along a ridge trail in the gray light of early morning. Colby tracked him for an hour and a half. Founder stayed close, ears forward, reading the air. Skunk hung back, a shadow among shadows, letting Colby work.

The shot was from forty yards. Colby steadied Judith against a forked branch, the way Skunk had taught him. He controlled his breathing. He set the front sight on the buck's shoulder, where the lungs were, where a clean kill lived. He squeezed the trigger the way Skunk had described — slow, steady, surprise yourself when it breaks.

The flint struck. The pan flashed. The rifle kicked against his shoulder. Through the smoke, Colby saw the buck stagger, take two steps, and fall.

He walked to it. The buck was dead — the shot had been clean, through the lungs, the animal down in seconds. It lay on its side in the leaves, its dark eye open, its rack catching the light. It was the largest animal Colby had ever been close to, and it was dead because he had put a ball through its lungs from forty yards, and the reality of that sat in his chest with a weight that was not guilt and was not pride but something between the two.

Responsibility. That was the word. He was responsible for this animal's death. Not Skunk. Not the trap. Not the mechanism of rope and wood. Colby's hands had loaded the rifle, Colby's eyes had found the track, Colby's finger had pulled the trigger. The buck was his. The kill was his. The meat and the hide and the antlers and the weight of all of it — his.

Skunk appeared beside him. He looked at the buck. He looked at the entry wound — clean, tight, exactly where it should be.

"Forty yards," Skunk said to Colby. "Lungs. One shot." He pulled his knife. "Let's get to work."

They dressed the buck in the field. Skunk showed Colby how to open the belly, remove the organs, prop the chest cavity with a stick to cool the meat. They quartered it and packed it on a frame of branches that Skunk built in ten minutes, and they carried it back to camp, Colby's shoulders burning under the weight, his legs steady beneath him, his moccasins gripping the frozen ground.

The venison lasted a week. The hide would become clothing or trade goods. The antlers would become tools. Nothing was wasted. In this world, waste was a sin worse than theft, because theft took from a person and waste took from the earth, and the earth was the only thing keeping everyone alive.

That evening, sitting by the fire, Skunk brought up the gathering.

"There's a rendezvous coming," Skunk said to Colby. He was stitching a tear in his moccasin with a bone needle and sinew, the firelight catching his fingers as they pulled the thread through the leather. "Four or five weeks. Down on the Licking River, same place they've held it the last ten years. Trappers, traders, a few families from the settlements. Sixty people, maybe more. It's where I trade my pelts for powder and lead and the few things I can't make myself."

Colby looked at the pelt rack. It was full now — not just Skunk's catch but Colby's too. Four beaver, six rabbit, three marten, and the deer hide from the buck. In a month and a half, Colby had gone from a boy who couldn't build a fire to a boy with his own pelts on the rack, and the sight of them hanging there in the firelight — stretched and scraped and ready for trade — was a sight that did something to his chest that he didn't have a word for.

"You'll come with me," Skunk said to Colby. It was not a question. "You'll trade your pelts. Whatever you get, you keep. That's yours. You trapped it, you skinned it, you earned it."

"What do they trade for?" Colby asked Skunk.

"Goods, mostly. Powder, lead, cloth, tools, salt. Some trade for gold when the traders have it. Gold's lighter than goods and it don't rot." Skunk bit the sinew and tied it off. "There'll be people there. First people you've seen besides me in two months. Some of them are decent. Some of them ain't. The decent ones will leave you alone. The ones that ain't will test you, because that's what men do when they see a boy they don't know — they test him to see what he's made of."

Colby thought about Trent. The testing. The daily measurement of what Colby would endure without pushing back. The frontier version would be different in form but the same in purpose — men finding the edges of a boy to see if the edges held.

"What do I do when they test me?" Colby asked Skunk.

Skunk set the moccasin down. He looked at Colby across the fire.

"You stand," Skunk said to Colby. "You don't start nothing. You don't run from nothing. You look them in the eye and you stand. A man who stands don't need to explain himself. His standing does the explaining."

He picked the moccasin back up. The needle went through the leather. The thread pulled tight.

"And I'll be there," Skunk said to Colby, quieter now, the voice closer to the voice he'd used when he'd talked about his wife and son on the Clinch River. "Anybody puts a hand on you, they'll answer for it. You got my word on that."

Colby felt something move in his chest. Not the stone-in-the-well feeling that Lloyd's "son" produced. Not the hand-on-the-shoulder feeling of Skunk's approval. Something different. Something that Colby had to search his memory to identify, because the last time he'd felt it, he was nine years old and his mother was married to a man who hadn't started drinking yet, and the world was still a place where adults could be trusted to keep a child safe.

Protection. The feeling of being protected. Not by a piece of paper in a kitchen drawer. Not by a restraining order that restrained nothing. By a man. A man who had looked at a lost boy in strange clothes and decided, without being asked and without expectation of repayment, that the boy was worth defending.

Colby stared at the fire. The flames reflected in the tears that he would not let fall, because Colby Utterback did not cry. But the reflection was there, shimmering, and Skunk saw it and said nothing, because Skunk knew that some things didn't need words. They just needed a fire and a dog and a man who kept his promises and the quiet of a forest that had been standing long enough to understand that the strongest things in the world were the ones that grew slowly.

Founder pressed closer against Colby's leg. The crooked tail settled. The fire crackled. And four or five weeks away, on the Licking River, sixty strangers were gathering, and Colby Utterback was going to walk among them with pelts to trade and a knife on his belt and a man at his back who had given his word.

For the first time since the storeroom, Colby was looking forward to something.

Chapter Seven - The Gathering

They walked for three days to reach the Licking River.

Skunk carried his pelts in a bundle on his back — two months' worth of beaver, marten, and deer hides, wrapped in oilcloth and strapped with rawhide, the pack riding high between his shoulder blades.

Colby carried his own — smaller, lighter, but his. Four beaver, six rabbit, three marten, and the buck hide. The weight of them pressed into his shoulders with every step, and the pressing felt good, the way carrying something you earned always feels different from carrying something you owe.

Founder ranged ahead of them, appearing and disappearing in the trees, chasing smells, investigating the private business of squirrels, occasionally returning to walk beside Colby for a stretch before the woods called him away again. The dog had opinions about the journey. The opinions were mostly positive.

Skunk talked more on the trail than he did in camp. The walking loosened something in him — stories came out, unconnected, offered without introduction and without moral, the way a man shares stories when he's been storing them for years and finally has someone to tell them to.

He told Colby about the first time he'd come to Kentuckee — alone, on foot, through the Cumberland Gap, with a rifle and a knife and sixty pounds of nothing useful on his back. He told him about a bear that had raided his camp three nights running and how he'd finally solved the problem by hanging his food from a branch so high the bear sat under it for an hour, looking up, with the expression of a creature reconsidering its life choices. He told him about Harlan Prewitt, the man who'd named him Skunk, who had died in a river crossing in "seventy-four and whose body was never found.

"Good man," Skunk said to Colby as they climbed a ridge on the second morning. "Best trapper I ever knew. Could read a track in the dark by feel. Lost his footing on a crossing in high water and the river took him. That's how it goes out here. You're alive and then the river decides you ain't, and there ain't no arguing with a river."

Colby listened. He listened the way he'd always listened — quietly, completely, storing the words the way Skunk stored pelts, each one stretched and saved for later use. Skunk's stories weren't lessons. They were the man himself, offered in pieces, and Colby accepted every piece.

They smelled the gathering before they saw it.

Wood smoke, heavy and layered — not the single thread of Skunk's fire but a cloud, the accumulated smoke of thirty or forty campfires burning at once. Under the smoke, meat. Under the meat, something sharper — the smell of tanned hides, of horses, of people living close together in a way that Colby hadn't experienced in over two months.

The forest thinned. The ground sloped downward toward a river bottom — flat, wide, the kind of ground that rivers make when they flood and retreat over centuries. The Licking River curved through the middle of it, shallow and broad, the water catching the December sunlight in flashes of white.

And on both banks, spread out across the flat ground like a temporary town, was the gathering.

Colby stopped walking. He stood at the tree line and looked.

He had expected something small. A few tents, a few men, a campfire. What he saw was a settlement. Lean-tos and canvas shelters and rough-built cabins lined the riverbank. Smoke rose from dozens of fires. Horses were tied to a picket line along the eastern edge, maybe twenty of them, and near the horses were wagons — three big ones with canvas tops and wooden sides, loaded with trade goods. People moved between the shelters, and the sound of them carried up the slope — voices, laughter, the ring of a hammer on metal, a dog barking, a child shouting.

People. Sixty or more. The most people Colby had seen since he'd left the storeroom.

His chest tightened. Not fear exactly — something more specific. The anticipation of being seen. In Skunk's camp, he was known. Skunk saw him and Founder saw him and the forest didn't care what he looked like. Down there, he'd be a stranger. A boy nobody recognized, wearing buckskins he hadn't owned two months ago, carrying pelts he'd trapped himself, with a crooked nose and the posture of someone who was still learning that his shoulders were allowed to be out.

Skunk stood beside him. He adjusted the pack on his back and looked down at the gathering with the expression of a man surveying a chore he'd rather skip.

"I hate this part," Skunk said to Colby.

"The gathering?" Colby asked Skunk.

"The people. Sixty of them, all talking at once, all wanting to trade, half of them drunk by noon. I do this twice a year because I need powder and lead, and the rest of the year I recover from the experience." He looked at Colby. "Stay close. Don't start nothing. And if somebody offers you whiskey, say no. The whiskey down there could strip the bark off a hickory, and you're fifteen."

They walked down the slope. Founder trotted beside Colby, ears forward, nose working, the dog reading the crowd from a hundred yards the way Colby read tracks.

The gathering was louder up close.

The noise hit Colby like a wall. After two months of forest silence — of creek water and bird calls and the low murmur of Skunk's voice — the sound of sixty people living and working and arguing and laughing was almost physical. His ears rang with it. His body tensed the way it used to tense when Arnold came through the front door, and he had to remind himself that the noise was not dangerous. It was just noise.

Men looked at them as they entered the camp. Colby felt the looks the way he'd always felt looks — on his skin, like heat. The men were rough, most of them — bearded, sun-darkened, dressed in buckskins or linen or combinations of both that had been worn until the original color was a memory. They carried knives and hatchets and a few carried rifles, and they looked at Skunk with the recognition of men who knew him and at Colby with the curiosity of men who didn't.

"Skunk!" A voice from the left. A man approached — shorter than Skunk, wider, with a red beard that spread across his chest like a bib. He was missing two fingers on his left hand and smiled like a man who'd lost them doing something he'd do again. "You old buzzard. Thought the Shawnee finally got you."

"Shawnee got better sense than to come after me," Skunk said to the man. "Whitley, this is Colby. He's with me."

Whitley looked at Colby. The look was quick, professional — the assessment of a man who measured people the way a trader measured pelts. He noted the buckskins, the knife on the belt, the pack of furs. He noted the youth and the crooked nose and the way the boy met his eyes without flinching.

"Yours?" Whitley asked Skunk, meaning kin.

"Mine," Skunk said to Whitley. The word landed without explanation, and the way Skunk said it closed the door on further questions. Mine. The boy is mine. That's all you need to know.

Whitley nodded. He stuck out his three-fingered hand. Colby shook it. The grip was strong and the missing fingers made the handshake feel strange and solid at the same time, like shaking hands with a tool.

"Welcome to the Licking, son," Whitley said to Colby. "Don't drink the whiskey. It'll kill your insides and insult your outsides."

Skunk led Colby through the camp. They found a spot on the south bank, upstream from the main cluster, and set up a lean-to and a fire with the efficiency of two people who had done it together enough times that the work divided itself without discussion. Colby built the fire. Skunk built the shelter. Founder lay between them and supervised.

The trading started the next morning.

A long table had been set up near the largest wagon — planks laid across sawhorses, covered with goods. Colby had never seen so many things in one place that weren't in a store. Gunpowder in kegs. Lead bars for casting balls. Bolts of cloth — linen, wool, a single bolt of something bright red that the traders handled like money. Knives, hatchets, iron pots, sewing needles, salt in linen bags, glass beads in jars. And beside the goods, a set of brass scales and a locked strongbox that Colby understood without being told held gold.

The trader behind the table was a man named Burnett.

Colby knew his type immediately, the way he knew Trent's type, the way he knew Arnold's type, the way a boy who has spent his life reading people for survival reads everyone he meets. Burnett was a big man — tall, heavy through the chest, with a clean-shaven face that stood out among the beards like a cleared field in a forest. He wore linen, not buckskin. His boots were leather, not moccasin. He had the hands of a man who handled goods, not tools — clean fingernails, soft palms, the hands of someone whose labor was negotiation.

But his eyes were sharp. The eyes of a man who had built something in a place that destroyed most of what people tried to build, and who had survived by seeing things clearly and acting on what he saw.

Burnett had a family. A wife — a quiet, sturdy woman who managed the second wagon and kept a ledger in handwriting so precise it looked printed. Seven children, ranging from a boy about Colby's age to a toddler who sat in the dirt near the wagon wheel chewing on a stick. The oldest boy — Burnett's son, maybe sixteen — worked the table beside his father, weighing pelts, marking prices, managing the flow of trappers who lined up to trade.

Skunk traded first. He laid his pelts on the table and Burnett examined them one by one — checking the quality of the scraping, the thickness of the fur, the size. The negotiation was short. Skunk knew what his pelts were worth and Burnett knew that Skunk knew, and the two men arrived at a number with the efficiency of people who had been doing this with each other for years. Burnett counted gold coins from the strongbox. Skunk pocketed them and bought powder and lead and a new piece of flint and a small bag of salt.

Then Skunk stepped aside and put his hand on Colby's shoulder.

"He's got his own," Skunk said to Burnett.

Burnett looked at Colby. The sharp eyes did their assessment. Colby laid his pelts on the table — the beaver, the marten, the rabbit, the buck hide. His hands were steady. His jaw was set. He was not nervous, because the pelts were good and he knew they were good, and a boy who has spent his life being told he's insufficient develops an acute sensitivity to the moments when he isn't.

Burnett examined the pelts. He took his time. The beaver were clean — well-scraped, properly stretched. The marten were small but the fur was dense. The rabbits were average. The buck hide was excellent — Skunk had supervised the scraping and Colby had done it right.

"Who taught you?" Burnett asked Colby, turning the buck hide in his hands.

"He did," Colby said to Burnett, nodding toward Skunk.

Burnett glanced at Skunk. Something passed between the two men — not a word, not a nod, just a recognition. Skunk had taught this boy, and the boy had learned well, and

Burnett was a man who respected the transfer of skill because his own livelihood depended on it.

"Two pounds six for the lot," Burnett said to Colby. "Gold or goods."

Colby looked at Skunk. Skunk gave a single, small nod. The nod meant: fair price.

"Gold," Colby said to Burnett.

Burnett counted the coins. He laid them on the table — small, heavy, gold catching the morning light. Colby picked them up. The weight of them in his palm was different from any weight he'd ever held. Not heavier than a twenty-dollar bill. Not lighter. Just different — the weight of something you earned with your hands and your time and your skill, paid by a man who didn't give charity and didn't overpay and had looked at your work and decided it was worth exactly this much.

Colby put the coins in his pouch. The leather pouch that Skunk had given him a week ago — small, drawstring, made from scrap deer hide. It was the first money Colby had earned that didn't come with a time clock or a shift schedule or a boss who said "Good job, son" in a tone that meant kindness but also meant pity.

This money meant: you can do this. You belong in these woods. Your work has value, and the man with the scales just proved it.

The gathering lasted four days.

Colby stayed close to Skunk the first day, watching. By the second day he was moving through the camp on his own, Founder at his side, the dog serving as both companion and early warning system. The trappers and their families treated Colby with the casual indifference of people who had seen enough strangers to not be bothered by one more, and the indifference was a gift. In Corbin, Colby had been visible in the worst way — the poor kid, the beat-up kid, the kid in the Goodwill jacket. Here, he was a boy in buckskins with a dog, same as half the boys at the gathering.

He watched the blacksmith shape an axe head on a portable forge, the hammer ringing in the cold air. He watched a woman tan a hide using a method different from Skunk's — brains instead of smoke, the hide turning soft and white. He watched two men settle a trade dispute with a footrace that ended in both of them falling into the river, which the crowd found hilarious and which the two men also found hilarious once they stopped coughing up water.

He ate food he'd never tasted — cornbread cooked on a stone, venison stew thick with wild onion and potato, a sweet paste made from dried persimmons that stuck to his teeth and tasted like the best thing a tree had ever produced. A woman with gray braids and a face like carved oak gave him a bowl of stew without asking his name or expecting anything in return, and Colby ate it standing near her fire and said thank you and the woman nodded and went back to her work, and the transaction was so simple and so kind that Colby had to look at the river for a moment until the burning behind his eyes went away.

Children ran through the camp — chasing each other, chasing dogs, getting underfoot and being yelled at and loved in the loud, careless way that frontier families loved their children. Colby watched them the way a person watches something they recognize from a distance. He'd never been those children. He'd never run through a camp without worrying about who was watching. But the sight of them running — free, unhurt, noisy with the noise of kids who weren't afraid — did something to the place in his chest where the weight usually sat. It lightened the weight. Not because the weight was gone, but because the world contained children who didn't carry one, and the existence of that possibility was enough to make his own weight feel less permanent.

The trouble came on the third evening.

Colby was at the edge of the camp, near the picket line where the horses were tied, throwing a stick for Founder. The dog had decided that retrieving was beneath him and was watching the stick land with the expression of a creature who understood the game and had chosen not to participate. Colby threw another stick. Founder watched it land. Colby was beginning to suspect that the dog was training him rather than the other way around.

A man appeared. Not from the main camp — from the direction of a smaller cluster of shelters on the far bank, where a group of trappers had set up apart from the rest. These men were louder than the others, drunker earlier in the day, and Skunk had told Colby to stay away from them without explaining why, which was explanation enough.

The man was big. Not tall-big — wide-big. Barrel-chested, thick-armed, with a beard that was black and matted and looked like it hadn't been washed since the previous gathering. He walked with the heavy, deliberate stride of a man who expected the ground to move for him, and his eyes were the dull, reddened eyes of someone who had been drinking since morning.

He stopped in front of Colby. He looked down at him. Colby was tall for fifteen, but this man had four inches and eighty pounds on him, and the eighty pounds were distributed in a way that suggested the man used them regularly on things that couldn't fight back.

"You're the Skunk's boy," the man said to Colby. It was not a question. The voice was thick with whiskey and the particular contempt of a man who had decided to dislike someone before meeting them.

Colby felt his body do the thing it always did. The tightening. The calculation. The rapid assessment of distance and position and escape route that Arnold had taught him without meaning to — the survival math that victims learn and never forget. The man was three feet away. The horses were behind Colby. The main camp was fifty yards to the left. Skunk was at their lean-to, maybe a hundred yards.

But the assessment was different now. In Corbin, the assessment ended with: don't move, don't speak, absorb it. Here, the assessment ended somewhere else. Colby didn't know where yet. But the ending was different.

"I'm with Skunk," Colby said to the man. His voice was even. Steady. The voice of a boy who had built fires and tracked deer and put a rifle ball through a buck's lungs at forty yards.

The man spat. The spit landed near Colby's moccasin.

"Skunk's a hermit and a fool," the man said to Colby. "Lives alone in the woods like an animal. Talks to a dog. Now he's got a boy doing his trapping for him. What's he paying you? Or is it the other kind of arrangement?"

The insult was clear. The insult was designed to do what Trent's insults were designed to do — to find the soft place and press on it, to make the target feel small, to establish that the man doing the talking owned the space and the boy being talked to did not.

Colby's jaw tightened. His hands stayed at his sides. He looked the man in the eyes — something he would not have done two months ago, something he could not have done two months ago, because two months ago his eyes were trained to look down and his body was trained to shrink and his voice was trained to say nothing.

But two months ago was a different boy in a different world, and this boy had a knife on his belt and calluses on his hands and the memory of Skunk saying

you stand.

"Skunk's not a fool," Colby said to the man. "And I'm not discussing him with you."

The man blinked. The blink was small but it was there — the micro-response of a bully who had expected submission and received something else. Colby recognized it because he had watched Trent blink the same way once, on a day when Colby had accidentally made eye contact for half a second too long and Trent's script had stuttered.

The man's face darkened. He stepped forward. His hand came up.

And then Founder was between them.

The dog had not been visible a second ago. Now he was standing between Colby and the man, his body low, his ears flat against his skull, his lips pulled back over teeth that were not impressive individually but were presented collectively with a conviction that made up for their size. The growl that came from Founder's chest was low and continuous, the sound of an engine idling, a sound that said: the next step you take will cost you.

The man looked at the dog. The dog looked at the man. The man's hand stayed up. The dog's lips stayed back.

"Call off your dog," the man said to Colby.

"He's not my dog to call off," Colby said to the man. "He makes his own decisions."

This was true. Founder was not a dog who took orders. Founder was a dog who made assessments and acted on them, and the assessment of the man in front of him was apparently unfavorable, because the growl deepened and the crooked tail went rigid and the oversized brown eyes locked on the man's face with an intensity that had nothing to do with the dog's usual mild disappointment in the world.

The man lowered his hand. He stepped backward. One step. Two. The retreat was slow and unconvincing — the man's face was tight with the anger of someone who had been outmaneuvered by a boy and a one-eared dog — but it was a retreat, and Colby watched it happen and felt something bloom in his chest that he had never felt before.

Not anger. Not relief. Something more fundamental than either. The feeling of holding ground. Of being in a space and refusing to leave it. Of looking a man in the eye and saying no, and meaning it, and the no being enough.

The man walked away. He didn't look back. Founder held his position for ten seconds after the man was gone, then relaxed — ears up, tail uncurling, lips settling back over the teeth. He turned to Colby and sat down and looked up at him with the brown eyes, and the look said: that's handled.

Colby knelt. He put his hands on both sides of Founder's face — the patchy fur, the one good ear, the one bad ear, the skull that was warm and solid between his palms.

"Good boy," Colby said to Founder. "Good boy."

Founder's crooked tail wagged. The wag was modest. But the eyes said: I know.

Colby didn't tell Skunk about the man.

Not because he was afraid. Because it was handled. The man had come, and Colby had stood, and Founder had stepped in, and the man had left. The equation was balanced. Telling Skunk would unbalance it — Skunk would go looking for the man, and looking for the man meant a confrontation that Colby didn't need, because the confrontation had already happened and Colby had come out of it standing.

He sat by the fire that night and looked at the coins in his pouch. Two pounds six. Gold. His. He added them up in his head — not their 1781 value but the feeling of them, the weight of competence, the evidence that his hands could produce something the world was willing to pay for.

Skunk was across the fire, whittling. Founder was against Colby's leg. The gathering hummed around them, sixty lives being lived within earshot, and Colby sat in the middle of all of it and felt, for the first time, like he was not watching from the window.

He was at the table.

Chapter Eight – Blood

The last morning of the gathering started quiet.

Colby was at the river, filling the water bucket. The sun was barely up — a thin line of orange along the ridge to the east, the rest of the sky still gray, the air cold enough that the water steamed where it met the bucket's rim. Founder sat on the bank behind him, watching the current with the detached interest of a dog who had no intention of getting wet but appreciated water as a concept.

The camp was waking up. Fires being restarted, voices low, the sounds of people shaking off sleep and whiskey and the fourth day of living too close together. Most of the trappers would leave today — pack their goods, break their shelters, disappear back into the woods they'd come from. The gathering was ending. By tomorrow, the flat ground along the Licking River would be empty except for the fire rings and the trampled grass and the memory of sixty people who had been there.

Colby carried the bucket back to camp. Skunk was crouched by the fire, feeding it sticks, his face lit orange in the early light. He looked tired. Four days of people had taken something out of him, the way four days of weather takes something out of a roof — not damaged, just worn down, ready for the quiet to come back.

"We'll leave after midday," Skunk said to Colby. "Sooner I'm back in my own woods, the sooner my ears stop ringing."

Colby set the bucket down. He poured water into the pot for tea. The routine was automatic now — water, fire, tea, the morning unfolding in the same order it had unfolded every morning for two and a half months. His hands knew the sequence. His body knew the rhythm. The boy who had stood in a storeroom in Corbin, Idaho, and didn't know how to build a fire was gone. The boy who replaced him could start a fire in four strikes, set a snare that caught dinner, track a deer through bare-branch December forest, and load a flintlock in under a minute.

The boy who replaced him had gold in his pouch and calluses on his hands and a dog who had chosen him and a man who had called him mine.

The morning should have stayed quiet. It didn't.

The man from the picket line came back.

Colby didn't see him coming. He was packing their pelts — the unsold ones, the ones Skunk was holding for the spring gathering when prices would be better — rolling them into the oilcloth bundle, tying the rawhide straps. Founder saw him first. The dog's head came up from his paws, ears locking forward, a low sound starting in his chest that was not yet a growl but was headed there.

Colby turned.

The man was twenty feet away and closing. He was not alone. Another man walked beside him — thinner, taller, with a face that looked like it had been assembled from spare parts and none of them matched. The thin man had a jug in his hand. The big man had nothing in his hands, but his right hand hung near his belt, and on his belt was a knife.

They were drunk. Both of them. Drunk at sunrise, which meant they had been drinking all night, and men who drank all night at a gathering did not come to another man's camp at dawn to trade pleasantries.

Colby stood up. His body did the math. The men were between him and the main camp. Skunk was behind him, by the fire. Judith was in the lean-to, too far to reach and too slow to load. The knife on Colby's belt was a skinning knife, short-bladed, meant for hides, not people.

The big man stopped ten feet from Colby. His face was red. The dull eyes from three nights ago were worse now — bloodshot, swollen, the eyes of a man who had marinated in whiskey until the whiskey had dissolved whatever thin layer of judgment had been sitting on top of the anger.

"Your dog bit Pruitt last night," the big man said to Colby. He pointed at the thin man. Pruitt held up his hand. There was a mark on it — red, swollen, broken skin. It might have been a dog bite. It might have been anything.

"Founder was with me all night," Colby said to the man. His voice was steady. His heart was not. "He didn't bite anybody."

"You calling Pruitt a liar?" the big man said to Colby.

The question was a door. Colby had seen this door before. Trent opened it with "Smelled your jacket from outside." Arnold opened it with "What did you say to me?" The words were different. The architecture was the same — a question designed so that every answer was wrong, because the question was never the point. The point was what came after.

Colby didn't answer. He stood. The way Skunk had told him to stand. Eyes level, shoulders out, weight balanced. He stood and waited for the man to show him what this was actually about.

The big man's hand moved to his belt. The movement was slow and deliberate and meant to be seen — the hand resting on the handle of the knife, the fingers curling around it, the message clear. The message said: I have a blade and you are a boy and this can go one of two ways.

Skunk's voice came from behind Colby.

"Take your hand off that knife, Jenks."

The voice was quiet. It was the quietest sound in the clearing. It was quieter than the fire and the river and the birds waking up in the trees. It was quiet the way a pulled-back hammer is quiet — the silence that comes right before the noise.

Skunk walked past Colby. He walked slowly, his hands at his sides, no weapon drawn. He stopped between Colby and the man — between Colby and the knife — and he stood there the way a wall stands, not because it's trying but because standing is what walls do.

Jenks looked at Skunk. Skunk looked at Jenks. The two men were roughly the same height. Skunk was older. Jenks was heavier. Neither of those facts mattered, because the thing that was happening between their eyes was not about size or age. It was about the question of who was willing to go further, and Skunk's eyes answered that question the way a cliff answers the question of whether it ends.

"The boy's dog didn't bite nobody," Skunk said to Jenks. "You know it and I know it. You came over here looking for something to break because you drank yourself mean last night and you need somebody smaller than you to take it out on. That ain't going to be this boy. Not today. Not any day while I'm breathing."

Jenks's face worked. The red deepened. The hand on the knife tightened.

"You're an old man, Skunk," Jenks said. "Don't make this about you."

"You made it about me when you walked into my camp with a knife and a lie and pointed both of them at my boy." Skunk's voice didn't rise. It didn't need to. "Walk away. Walk away now and this ends here and nobody gets hurt and tomorrow we all go back to our woods and forget this happened."

For one second, Colby thought it was over. Jenks's hand loosened on the knife. His eyes dropped. The thin man — Pruitt — took a half step backward, the retreat of a man who had signed up for intimidation and was seeing the contract renegotiated in real time.

Then Jenks pulled the knife.

It happened fast.

Not movie-fast — not the choreographed slow-motion of a fight scene where every movement is visible and makes sense. Real-fast. Ugly-fast. The fast of a thing that nobody planned and nobody controlled and that happened in the space between one heartbeat and the next.

Jenks pulled the knife and swung it at Skunk. Not a stab — a wild, drunken slash, the blade cutting the air at chest height, the motion of a man who had reached the bottom of his judgment and found violence waiting there. Skunk stepped back. The blade missed his chest. It did not miss his arm.

The knife caught Skunk on the outside of his left forearm, just below the elbow. The cut was long and deep — Colby saw the buckskin sleeve open and the skin underneath open with it, and the blood came immediately, dark red, running down Skunk's forearm and over his hand and dripping from his fingers onto the ground.

Skunk didn't make a sound. His right hand came up and hit Jenks in the face — not a punch, an open-handed strike, the heel of his palm connecting with the bridge of Jenks's nose with a crack that sounded like a branch breaking. Jenks staggered. The knife dropped. Skunk hit him again — same hand, same spot — and Jenks went down, hitting the ground the way large men hit the ground, all at once, the weight of him shaking the earth.

Pruitt ran. He turned and ran toward the far bank without looking back, the jug still in his hand, the retreat of a man who had seen the future and wanted no part of it.

Skunk stood over Jenks. His left arm hung at his side. The blood ran freely — not spurting, not the bright arterial spray that meant the worst, but a steady, heavy flow that was soaking the buckskin and pooling in the dirt. Skunk's face was white. Not pale — white. The color of a man who was losing blood fast enough that his body was starting to reroute.

He took one step. His knee buckled. He caught himself. He took another step and the knee buckled again and this time he didn't catch himself.

Skunk went down.

Colby was on the ground beside him before the man's back hit the dirt.

He didn't think. Thinking would have been too slow and too complicated and would have involved the part of his brain that was screaming that this was wrong, that Skunk was supposed to be the one who was unbreakable, the wall, the man who stood between Colby and the knife, and walls weren't supposed to bleed. Thinking would have frozen him. So he didn't think. He acted.

He grabbed Skunk's left arm. The blood was hot on his hands — hotter than he expected, the heat of a living thing leaving a living body, and the heat was the thing that made it real, because you could see blood in a movie or a video game and feel nothing, but you could not feel the heat of another person's blood on your hands and feel nothing.

The cut was six inches long, running from below the elbow to the middle of the forearm. It was deep. Colby could see the muscle underneath, dark red and glistening, and beneath the muscle, the pale glint of something harder. Bone, maybe. Or tendon. He didn't know. He didn't need to know. He needed to stop the bleeding.

He ripped the sleeve off his buckskin shirt. The leather was tough but his hands were stronger than they'd been two months ago and the stitching gave way. He folded the sleeve into a pad and pressed it against the wound — hard, both hands, the way he'd seen it done on television once and the way instinct told him to do it now. Press and hold. Press and hold. Don't lift. Don't look. Press and hold.

"Colby." Skunk's voice was thin. Thinner than Colby had ever heard it — the deep, rough, unhurried voice reduced to something papery and small, the voice of a man whose body was telling him to shut down and save what was left.

"Shut up," Colby said to Skunk.

He said it without deciding to. He said it the way Skunk said things — directly, without performance, because the situation was too urgent for manners. Skunk needed to stop talking and Colby needed to keep pressing and the blood needed to stop coming, and those were the only three facts in the world right now.

Skunk shut up.

People were coming. Colby heard them — voices, footsteps, the sound of the gathering waking up to a fight it had missed. Whitley was the first to arrive. He took one look at Skunk on the ground and Colby pressing the leather pad against the arm and the blood soaking through and the boy's face, which was the face of someone who was holding the world together with two hands and was not going to let go.

"How bad?" Whitley asked Colby.

"Deep," Colby said to Whitley. "Long. Bleeding heavy. I'm pressing on it."

"Keep pressing," Whitley said to Colby. He knelt on Skunk's other side. "Somebody get Burnett's wife. She's got a needle and thread and she's sewed up worse than this."

Colby pressed. The leather pad was soaked through. He could feel the pulse of Skunk's blood against his palms — steady but weaker, the rhythm slowing, the engine running down. He pressed harder. His arms shook. He pressed anyway.

"You're hurting me, boy," Skunk said to Colby. The voice was barely there.

"Good," Colby said to Skunk. "That means you're alive."

Founder was at Skunk's head. The dog had not barked, had not growled, had not done any of the things a dog does when its person is in danger. Instead, Founder had laid down next to Skunk's head and pressed his nose against the man's cheek, and the gesture was so human and so helpless and so full of the wordless love of a creature that could not fix the thing that was breaking but would not leave the side of the thing that was breaking — that Colby's eyes burned and his throat closed and he pressed harder on the wound because pressing was the only thing he could do and he was going to do it until his arms broke or the bleeding stopped or the world ended, whichever came first.

Burnett's wife came. Her name was Margaret. She was calm the way the river was calm — the surface still while the current underneath moved with purpose. She carried a leather roll that she opened to reveal needles, thread, strips of clean linen, and a stoppered bottle that smelled like whiskey.

"Let me see," Margaret said to Colby.

Colby lifted the pad. The bleeding had slowed — not stopped, but slowed, the steady flow reduced to a seep. Margaret looked at the wound. Her face showed nothing.

"You kept him alive," Margaret said to Colby. She said it as a fact, not a compliment. The same way a woman who had raised seven children on the frontier and sewed up knife wounds before breakfast stated facts — plainly, without embellishment, because the truth didn't need decoration.

She cleaned the wound with whiskey. Skunk's body jerked. His teeth clenched. The sound he made was not a scream — Skunk would not scream — but a low, animal groan that came from somewhere below language.

She sewed him up. Twenty-two stitches. Colby counted them, because counting was what he did when the world was too large to hold — he made it small, he made it numbers, he put it in rows. Twenty-two stitches. Each one a puncture and a pull and a knot, and Skunk lay still for every one of them, his eyes closed, his breathing shallow, Founder's nose against his cheek.

When it was done, Margaret wrapped the arm in clean linen and tied it off. She looked at Colby. The boy was kneeling in the dirt with blood on his hands and blood on his shirt and blood on his face where he'd pushed his hair back without thinking, and his hands were shaking now, shaking the way they hadn't shaken when they needed to be still, because the body waits until the crisis is over before it falls apart.

"You did right," Margaret said to Colby. "The pressure. The pad. You did exactly right."

Colby looked at his hands. They were red. Skunk's blood. The blood of the man who had fed him and taught him and given him moccasins and called him mine and stood between him and a knife. The blood was drying now, tightening on his skin, and Colby looked at it and thought about another night when there had been blood — his own blood, on a kitchen floor, pooling around his head while Arnold sat on the couch and opened another beer.

That blood had meant: nobody is coming for you.

This blood meant: I came for him.

Skunk slept for most of the day.

Colby sat beside him. He didn't leave. He didn't eat. He didn't walk to the river or check the fire or do any of the hundred things that made up a normal day, because none of those things were important and the only thing that was important was the man lying on the deerskin with twenty-two stitches in his arm and a dog pressed against his side.

People came and went. Whitley brought food. Colby didn't eat it. Burnett came by, looked at Skunk, looked at Colby, and left without speaking. A woman Colby didn't know left a pot of broth near the fire. Another man brought a blanket.

Whitley came back in the early afternoon. He crouched beside Colby and kept his voice low, the way men keep their voices low near the injured and the sleeping.

"We caught Jenks on the north trail," Whitley said to Colby. "Me and Burnett and three others. He didn't get far. Drunk and stupid is a slow combination."

Colby looked at Whitley. The three-fingered hand was resting on his knee. The knuckles were scraped.

"What happened?" Colby asked Whitley.

"The gathering held a council while you were sitting here. Didn't take long. Sixty people saw him pull a knife on a man with his hands down. That ain't a fight. That's attempted murder." Whitley spat to the side. "We took his pelts. Every one. A whole season's work. That's the fine for pulling a blade at a gathering. He's banned. Permanent. If he shows his face at the Licking River again, or any rendezvous in Kentuckee, the next council won't be a conversation."

"And Pruitt?" Colby asked Whitley.

"Pruitt gave up Jenks before we asked. Told us the whole thing was Jenks's idea, the dog bite was a lie, said he'd been afraid to say no." Whitley's face showed what he thought of that excuse. "Pruitt's banned too. One year. He can come back if somebody vouches for him, and good luck finding that somebody."

Whitley looked at Skunk sleeping. The bandaged arm. The color that still hadn't come all the way back to his face.

"Jenks's pelts will be split among the gathering," Whitley said to Colby. "But Skunk gets first cut. When he's up, he picks what he wants. That's the ruling."

Colby nodded. The justice was rough and fast and nothing like the courtroom Uncle James had taken him to, where a judge sat behind a desk and asked Wanda to press charges and Wanda wouldn't because the system was too slow and Arnold was too close. This justice was sixty men deciding in an afternoon that a wrong had been done and the wrong would be answered, and the answer was delivered before the sun went down, and the man who'd done the wrong was already gone with nothing in his hands and nowhere left to trade.

It wasn't perfect. But it was done.

Colby sat. He watched Skunk's chest rise and fall. He counted the breaths.

The counting had started with Carl. The small body on the couch, the wheezing, the thumb that told Colby whether his brother was okay. Then Founder — the ribs expanding and contracting against Colby's leg, the count that meant the dog was still there. Now Skunk. The chest rising under the deerskin, the breath shallow but steady, each one a promise that the next one was coming.

Three lives. Three sets of breathing. Three things Colby had appointed himself to watch over, not because anyone had asked him to, but because watching over things was the only skill he'd brought from his old life that mattered in this one.

Skunk opened his eyes near sunset. The gray eyes found Colby's face. The gaze was weak but clear.

"You still here?" Skunk asked Colby.

"I'm still here," Colby said to Skunk.

Told you to shut up earlier," Skunk said to Colby. "You told me to shut up. I told you to shut up," Colby said to Skunk.

Skunk's beard moved. The half-second rearrangement. The almost-smile.

"Fair enough." Skunk looked at his bandaged arm. He looked at the blood on Colby's hands and shirt. He looked at Founder, who had not moved from his side all day. "Jenks?"

"Gone," Colby said to Skunk. "Left this morning."

"Should have hit him harder," Skunk said to Colby. "You hit him pretty hard," Colby said to Skunk.

"Not hard enough. He's still got teeth." Skunk tried to sit up. The color left his face. He lay back down. "We're not leaving today."

"We're not leaving until you can walk," Colby said to Skunk. "I don't care if it takes a week."

Skunk looked at Colby. The look was long and quiet and held something that Colby had never seen in the man's face before — not approval, not the reading-the-story look, not the practical assessment of a teacher watching a student. Something else. Something that sat below all of those things, in the place where Skunk kept the things he didn't say out loud.

"You kept me alive," Skunk said to Colby.

"You stood in front of a knife for me," Colby said to Skunk.

The fire crackled. The river murmured. Founder's tail twitched against Skunk's hip.

"Reckon we're even, then," Skunk said to Colby.

They were not even. They would never be even. What had happened that morning was not a transaction that could be balanced — it was a bond, the kind that forms when one person bleeds for another and the other person presses his hands against the wound and refuses to let go. It was the kind of bond that Colby had never had with anyone, not with Wanda, not with Uncle James, not with any of the people in his life who had tried to help him and failed or tried to hurt him and succeeded.

Skunk had stood in front of a knife. For him. For a boy he'd known two and a half months. A boy who had walked out of the woods in strange shoes and couldn't build a fire.

And Colby had pressed his hands against the wound and held them there until the bleeding stopped and the stitches went in and the man who had called him mine was still breathing.

Colby looked at his hands. The blood was still there, dried to a dark brown, cracked in the lines of his palms. He could wash it off. He would wash it off, later, in the river. But right now it was proof. Proof that he had done something that mattered more than stacking shelves or putting twenties on a table.

He had kept someone alive.

The stars came out. Colby sat beside Skunk and counted his breaths, and the counting was steady, and the fire burned, and the gathering was quiet, and somewhere in the dark, Jenks was walking away from the Licking River with a broken nose and the knowledge that the old hermit and the boy and the one-eared dog were not to be tested again.

Skunk couldn't walk for three days.

The blood loss had taken more out of him than the cut. His face stayed pale. His hands trembled when he tried to lift the water cup. He slept in stretches — two hours, three, then awake and irritable, then asleep again, his body cycling through the slow, stubborn process of rebuilding what Jenks's knife had drained.

Margaret came twice a day to check the stitches. She cleaned the wound with whiskey and rewrapped the linen and told Skunk to stay down, and Skunk told Margaret that he'd been taking care of himself for thirty years and didn't need a nursemaid, and Margaret told Skunk that if he stood up before she said he could she'd sew his moccasins to the deerskin while he slept.

Skunk stayed down.

Colby ran the camp.

He didn't ask permission. He didn't announce it. He woke before dawn on the first morning after the stabbing and built the fire and boiled the tea and checked the snares and came back with two rabbits and gutted them and cooked one and set the other aside for later, and by the time Skunk opened his eyes, the camp was running the way it always ran — the fire steady, the water fresh, the food cooking — except the hands doing the running were fifteen years old instead of fifty-eight.

Skunk watched from the deerskin. His gray eyes tracked Colby's movements around the camp the way they'd tracked deer in the forest — quietly, missing nothing.

"You're banking the fire wrong," Skunk said to Colby on the second morning.

"The fire's burning fine," Colby said to Skunk.

"It's burning. It ain't banked. There's a difference. Push the coals to the left. The draft comes from the right. You want the heat to hold, not to blow."

Colby pushed the coals to the left. The fire settled. The heat deepened.

"You could have told me that from a lying-down position without the attitude," Colby said to Skunk.

"The attitude is free," Skunk said to Colby. "Consider it part of the education."

By the third day, Skunk was sitting up. By the fourth, he was standing, leaning against the rock face behind the lean-to, his left arm held close to his body, the bandage showing below the torn sleeve of his buckskin shirt. He looked diminished — not smaller exactly, but reduced, the way a fire looks reduced after a rain. Still burning. But quieter.

On the fifth morning, he told Colby they were leaving.

The walk back took four days instead of three.

Skunk moved slower. He wouldn't admit it — his legs kept the same pace, his moccasins hit the ground with the same rhythm, but the pauses were longer. He stopped to drink more often. He rested at the top of ridges with his back against a tree and his eyes closed, and the resting was not the resting of a man who was tired but the resting of a man whose body was spending energy on healing and had less to spend on walking.

Colby carried both packs. His own pelts and Skunk's — including the pick from Jenks's confiscated furs, four prime beaver that Skunk had chosen with one hand while leaning on Colby's shoulder with the other. The combined weight pressed into Colby's back and shoulders, and the pressing hurt, and he didn't mention it, and Skunk didn't ask.

They didn't talk much on the trail. The silence between them had changed since the stabbing. Before, the silence had been comfortable — the quiet of two people who didn't need words. Now the silence was heavier. It held something that neither of them had named, the weight of a thing that had happened between them that was too large for the small words that men on the frontier used.

Founder walked between them. The dog had not left Skunk's side since the stabbing, except to range ahead on the trail and come back, range ahead and come back, checking the path and then checking the man, the rhythm of an animal that had decided its job was to keep both of its people safe and was taking the job seriously.

On the second night, camped in a hollow below a sandstone ledge, Skunk spoke.

"I need to say something to you," Skunk said to Colby.

Colby was feeding the fire. He looked up. Skunk was sitting against the ledge with the deerskin over his legs and his injured arm cradled in his lap. The firelight made the lines on his face deeper, the gray of his beard more silver. He looked old. Not the weathered-old that Colby had gotten used to — a different old. The old of a man who had been reminded that his body was not permanent.

"I should have seen Jenks coming," Skunk said to Colby. "I knew what he was. I knew what he'd done to you at the picket line —"

"How did you know about that?" Colby asked Skunk.

"Whitley told me. The night it happened. You think a thing like that happens at a gathering and I don't hear about it?" Skunk's voice was rough with something that wasn't anger. "I should have gone to Jenks that night. Should have put myself between him and you before there was a knife in it. I waited, and the waiting cost me an arm's worth of blood and twenty-two stitches."

Colby set the stick down. "You did put yourself between him and me," Colby said to Skunk. "That's exactly what you did. You walked right past me and stood there with your hands down and told him to walk away. That's what you promised you'd do and that's what you did."

"Should have been sooner."

"Skunk." Colby's voice was firm. Firmer than he'd ever spoken to the man. "I have spent my whole life around a man who hit me and a system that didn't stop him. My uncle took me to a judge. The judge asked my mother to press charges. She wouldn't. Nobody stood in front of anything for me. Nobody. Until you."

The fire popped. A shower of sparks rose and died in the dark.

"So don't sit there and tell me you should have done it sooner," Colby said to Skunk. "You did it. That's more than anyone else ever did."

Skunk was quiet for a long time. The fire burned. Founder sighed from his spot between them, the sigh of a dog who was listening to a conversation he couldn't understand but could feel.

"You sound like my wife," Skunk said to Colby. His voice was quieter now. Closer to the voice he used when he talked about the Clinch River. "She had that same way of telling me I was wrong about being wrong. Made me feel like a fool for apologizing."

"Was she right?" Colby asked Skunk.

"Always," Skunk said to Colby. "Every single time."

They reached camp on the fourth afternoon.

Everything was as they'd left it. The lean-to stood. The fire pit was cold but undisturbed. The pelt rack was empty — they'd taken everything to the gathering — but the frame was solid, waiting. Colby's sneakers still sat near the fire pit where he'd left them two and a half months ago, dried and stiff and curling at the edges, relics from a world that felt further away every day.

Colby built the fire. Skunk lowered himself onto his stump and sat there with his arm in his lap and watched the camp come back to life under the boy's hands. The water boiled. The tea steeped. The rhythm returned.

"The camp is yours," Skunk said to Colby.

Colby looked at Skunk across the fire. "What do you mean?" Colby asked Skunk.

"I mean what I said. I'm going to be one-armed for a while. Weeks, maybe longer. Margaret said the muscle's cut deep and it'll heal slow. Which means I can't trap, can't chop, can't skin. Which means you do it." He looked at Colby with the gray eyes that missed nothing. "The trap line's yours. The hunting's yours. The firewood, the water, the cooking, the hides — yours. Everything we need to survive winter in these woods comes from your hands now. Can you do that?"

The question was real. Not a test, not a teaching moment. A real question from a man who needed a real answer because his survival depended on it. Skunk had never asked Colby a question like this before — every other lesson had been offered freely, the teaching of a man who enjoyed teaching. This was different. This was need.

"Yes," Colby said to Skunk.

He said it without hesitation. Not because he was certain — certainty was a luxury that Colby had never been able to afford — but because the alternative was useless. Skunk was hurt. Winter was coming. The camp needed running. Uncertainty was a feeling, and feelings didn't chop wood or check snares or keep a man with twenty-two stitches in his arm alive through December.

"Yes," Colby said to Skunk again, because some words need to be said twice to become real. "I can do that."

Winter came hard.

The first real snow fell three days after they returned

to camp. Not the dusting they'd had in November — a heavy, wet, serious snow that blanketed the forest in white and turned the creek banks to ice and dropped the temperature to a cold that Colby felt in his teeth. Idaho had winter. Corbin sat at four thousand feet and the snow came every year and stayed until March. But Idaho winters had furnaces and insulated walls and coats from the Goodwill rack that were at least designed for cold.

This winter had a fire, a lean-to, and buckskins.

Colby worked. He worked the way he'd always worked — steadily, without complaint, the rhythm of a body that had been trained to keep moving regardless of what the mind thought about it. He woke in the dark. He broke the ice on the water bucket. He built the fire high — higher than Skunk usually built it, because the cold was deeper than anything Colby had felt and the heat had to be bigger to fight it. He checked the trap line in snow that reached his knees in places, his moccasins wrapped in extra deer hide that Skunk had shown him how to tie before the arm gave out, his tracks the only marks in a white world.

The snares produced. Not every day — some days the trap line came up empty and Colby walked the circuit in silence and came back with nothing and the nothing felt like failure until Skunk told him that empty traps were part of trapping and that a man who expected every trap to catch was a man who didn't understand animals or odds.

"The woods don't owe you dinner," Skunk said to Colby from his stump by the fire. "You ask. Sometimes the answer's yes. Sometimes it ain't. Either way, you go back tomorrow and ask again."

Most days the answer was yes. Colby brought in rabbits, marten, a fox whose red pelt was so bright against the snow that he saw it from fifty yards and thought for one disoriented second that the forest was bleeding. He skinned them and stretched the hides and added them to the rack, and the rack filled steadily, and each pelt was a mark on a ledger that Colby was keeping in his head — not a money ledger, though the pelts would be money eventually, but a competence ledger. A record of days when his hands had done what needed doing.

He hunted alone. Skunk couldn't come — the arm wouldn't allow the long walks, the crouching, the steadiness needed to aim a rifle. Colby took Judith and Founder and went into the white forest and tracked deer through snow that told their story more clearly than bare ground ever had — every step printed, every pause visible, every place where the animal had stopped to browse or listen or test the air written in white like a letter from the woods to anyone who could read it.

He killed a doe in January — alone, no fawn this time, the animal standing in a clearing of birch trees, her brown body stark against the white. The shot was clean. Forty yards. Lungs. She fell where she stood. Colby dressed her in the field, his hands red to the wrists, the steam rising from the open body into the frozen air. He quartered her and packed the meat and dragged it back to camp on a frame of branches that he'd built himself without Skunk's help, and when he came into the clearing with the meat on his back and Founder trotting beside him, Skunk was standing by the fire with his good arm raised.

Not waving. Waiting. The posture of a man who had been listening for the rifle shot and had been counting the hours since, and had spent those hours doing the only thing a man with one working arm could do for a boy in the woods — standing by the fire and being there when he came back.

"Big doe," Skunk said to Colby.

"Big doe," Colby said to Skunk.

They didn't need more words than that. The meat was proof. The boy who'd walked out of a storeroom in sneakers and a polo shirt three months ago had just brought home a deer by himself in the dead of winter, and the man who'd taught him everything he knew was standing by the fire with pride on his face that even thirty years of frontier stoicism couldn't completely hide.

Skunk's arm healed slowly.

By late January, the stitches were out — Margaret's work holding, the wound closed to a raised pink scar that ran from below his elbow to mid-forearm. The muscle underneath was weak. Skunk could grip but not squeeze, lift but not carry, hold the hatchet but not swing it with the force that chopping demanded. He worked at it — flexing, gripping a stick, squeezing a ball of rawhide that Colby made for him — with the same patient, repetitive stubbornness that he applied to everything.

"It'll come back," Skunk said to Colby one evening, working the rawhide ball with his left hand, the fingers opening and closing in a rhythm that was slower than it should have been. "Muscle remembers. Takes its time, but it remembers."

"Like leather," Colby said to Skunk.

Skunk looked at him. The gray eyes held the almost-smile.

"Like leather," Skunk said to Colby.

February came. The snow deepened. The cold intensified. Colby ran the trap line and hunted and chopped wood and hauled water and kept the fire burning through nights so cold that the sap in the trees cracked like rifle shots in the dark. He fell into a rhythm that was deeper than routine — it was the rhythm of the land itself, the cycle of cold and work and rest that the forest had been running since before people were here to notice it, and Colby was inside the cycle now, part of it, his body rising and working and sleeping in time with the turning of a world that didn't know or care that he was from somewhere else.

He was not from somewhere else anymore.

He was from here. From this camp, this fire, this lean-to, this man, this dog. The storeroom and Corbin and Idaho were still inside him — Carl's breathing, Wanda's shoulders, the table and the twenty and the shame — but they were inside him the way Skunk's Virginia was inside Skunk. A place he came from. Not a place he was.

The place he was stood in moccasins in the snow with a rifle in his hands and a dog at his side and a scar on his heart where a man named Skunk had bled for him, and the place he was felt, for the first time in Colby Utterback's fifteen years, like home.

Chapter Ten – Thaw

March came like a promise the forest had been keeping.

The snow didn't leave all at once. It pulled back in stages — the south-facing slopes first, the brown earth showing through in patches like skin through a torn shirt, then the ridge tops, then the hollows where the cold held on longest. The creek, which had been a whisper under ice for two months, broke open and ran fast and loud, swollen with melt, carrying branches and leaves and the accumulated debris of a winter that had gone on long enough.

The birds came back. Colby heard them before he saw them — new songs in the canopy, songs that hadn't been there since November, the sound of the forest restocking itself. Skunk named them without looking up from whatever his hands were doing. Warbler. Thrush. Tanager. He knew them the way he knew trees and tracks and the weather — by sound, by feel, by thirty years of paying attention.

The air softened. Not warm yet — the mornings were still cold enough to freeze the water bucket — but the edge was gone, the killing edge that had turned January into a war between the fire and the dark. Colby could stand outside the lean-to in the early light without his body clenching against the cold, and the not-clenching was a kind of freedom he hadn't known he'd been missing until it came back.

Spring meant work. Different work. Winter work had been survival — keep the fire burning, keep the food coming, keep Skunk alive. Spring work was building. Skunk's arm was functional now — not full strength, the grip still weaker on the left than the right, the scar tissue pulling when he extended the arm too far — but functional enough to swing the hatchet, to set traps, to do the hundred things that two hands did better than one.

The camp expanded. Skunk showed Colby how to reinforce the lean-to with fresh poles, lashing them in place with strips of green bark that would shrink as they dried and tighten the joints. They built a smoking rack — a frame of green wood over a shallow pit where a slow fire could burn for days, the smoke curing meat and hides and turning perishable things into things that lasted. They dug a cold cellar — a hole three feet deep, lined with flat stones, covered with a slab of bark, a place to store meat out of the sun and away from the animals that would smell it.

Colby dug the cellar. It took two days. The ground was still half-frozen, and the digging was the hardest physical work he'd done since scraping his first hide — his shoulders burned, his back ached, his hands blistered through the calluses. He dug anyway. He dug because the cellar needed digging and his hands were the hands available, and by now the connection between need and work was so direct in Colby's body that it bypassed his brain entirely. Something needed doing. He did it. The equation was that simple, and the simplicity of it was the most valuable thing Kentucky had taught him.

Skunk started teaching again.

Not the basic lessons of the first months — fire, water, snares. Harder things. Things that took time and patience and the kind of hands-on repetition that couldn't be rushed.

He taught Colby to make rope. Not the rough twist that Colby had learned in the fall — real rope, made from the inner bark of a basswood tree, stripped and soaked and separated into fibers and twisted into cordage that was strong enough to hold a deer and flexible enough to coil. The process took days. The fibers had to be processed, dried, twisted in pairs, then twisted again in the opposite direction so the strands locked against each other. Colby's fingers cramped. The twisting was repetitive and precise and unforgiving — too tight and the rope was brittle, too loose and it had no strength.

"Rope is patience," Skunk said to Colby, watching the boy's fingers work. "Every twist has to be the same as the one before it. You can't hurry it. You can't skip a step. The rope don't care if you're tired or bored or your fingers hurt. The rope only cares if you did it right."

He taught Colby to read the weather. Not the basic signs — dark sky means rain, red sky at morning means trouble — but the deeper reading, the language of clouds and wind and pressure that told a man what was coming before it arrived. Skunk could feel a storm three days out. He said the air changed — the weight of it, the way it sat on the skin, the way the animals behaved. Deer moved to low ground before a storm. Birds went quiet. Founder would press close to the fire and refuse to range, his body curling tight, his nose tucked under his tail.

"The animals know before we do," Skunk said to Colby. "They feel what we have to think about. When the deer head for the hollows and the birds stop singing and that dog won't leave the fire, you pay attention. Something's coming."

He taught Colby to navigate. Not with a compass — Skunk didn't have a compass, didn't trust them, said a man who needed a needle in a box to find north was a man who hadn't been paying attention. He taught by landmarks — the bent oak on the ridge, the rock face shaped like a bear's head, the creek that ran east until it hit the sandstone shelf and turned south. He taught by sun and stars. He taught by moss, which grew thickest on the north side of trees, and by the lean of the hemlocks, which tilted south toward the light.

"You get lost in these woods, you die," Skunk said to Colby. "Simple as that. The forest don't send search parties.

You navigate or you wander, and men who wander in Kentuckee become bones that other men find in the spring."

Colby absorbed it. His pattern-recognition brain — the brain that counted heads and calculated rent and read Trent's body language in the hallway — turned out to be built for navigation the same way it was built for tracking. The forest was a system. The landmarks were data points. The sun and stars were coordinates. The moss and the tree lean were calibration tools. Colby's brain mapped the territory the way it mapped everything — automatically, quietly, building a model of the world that grew more detailed and more accurate every day.

By April, Colby could walk the trap line blindfolded. He could find camp from any ridge within five miles. He could point north without looking at the sky, the direction living in his body the way the fire-starting sequence lived in his hands — automatic, permanent, his.

The pelt rack was full.

Spring trapping was the best trapping. The animals were active after winter — moving, eating, rebuilding the fat they'd burned through the cold months. The beaver were thick-furred and plentiful. The marten were bold. Even the foxes, cautious in winter, made mistakes in spring, and Colby's snares caught three in two weeks.

Colby counted the pelts the way he counted

everything. Twenty-six beaver. Fourteen marten. Eleven fox. Eight rabbit. Three deer hides. The numbers were his — not Skunk's. Skunk had his own catch, smaller this year because of the arm, but Colby's rack was full, and the fullness of it was a thing Colby looked at every morning the way he used to look at the $80 on the kitchen table, except this time the looking didn't come with shame.

This time the looking came with a feeling he was still learning to name. The feeling of enough. Not enough in the way that Wanda's paycheck was never enough — not the desperate, temporary enough that lasted until the next bill arrived. A different enough. The enough of a person who had gone into the woods with nothing and come out with something that he'd built with his own time and skill and sweat, and the something was real and the something was his.

Skunk noticed the counting. He noticed everything.

"You're adding it up," Skunk said to Colby one evening, watching the boy's eyes move across the rack.

"I'm always adding it up," Colby said to Skunk.

"What's it add up to?" Skunk asked Colby.

Colby didn't answer right away. He looked at the rack. Twenty-six beaver alone would bring good money at the gathering. Beaver was the standard — the currency of the frontier, the pelt that every trader wanted, the fur that bought powder and lead and gold.

"More than I've ever had," Colby said to Skunk.

"More than most grown men bring to a gathering," Skunk said to Colby. "And you're fifteen." He was quiet for a moment. "The spring gathering's in six weeks. Same place, Licking River. Bigger than the winter one — eighty, maybe a hundred people. More traders, more goods, better prices." He paused. "You ready for that?"

Colby thought about Jenks. The knife. The blood. The hand on his belt and the spit near his moccasin. He thought about Burnett's table and the gold coins and the weight of them in his palm.

"I'm ready," Colby said to Skunk.

Skunk nodded. He picked up his whittling. The knife moved against the hickory in slow, even curls.

"This time you walk in different," Skunk said to Colby. "Last time you were new. Nobody knew you. This time they know you. They know what happened with Jenks. They know you sat with me while Margaret sewed my arm. They know you ran this camp through winter with a one-armed man and a one-eared dog and came out the other side with a full rack." He looked at Colby. "You ain't the strange boy in the strange shoes anymore. You're Skunk's boy. And in these woods, that means something."

Colby felt the words settle into the place where Skunk's words always settled — the place that had been empty for fifteen years and was filling now, one sentence at a time, the way a well fills after a long drought.

Six weeks. Then the gathering. Then the gold that would go into his pouch and add to the coins already there and become something more than money — something that a boy could carry through a gap in a rock wall and lay on a kitchen table in a house in Corbin, Idaho, and change the equation that had never balanced.

Six weeks.

Colby looked at the pelt rack. He looked at Skunk. He looked at Founder, who was chewing on a stick with the focused dedication of a dog who had found his life's work.

He was ready.

Chapter Eleven - The River

The spring gathering was twice the size of the winter one.

Colby saw it from the ridge above the Licking River and stopped walking. The flat ground along both banks was covered — shelters, fires, wagons, horses, people moving in every direction. The winter gathering had been sixty people. This was a hundred, maybe more, spread along a quarter mile of riverbank, and the noise of them carried up the slope like the sound of a town that had appeared overnight and would disappear just as fast.

More wagons this time — six or seven, loaded heavy, their canvas tops bright against the green of the new grass. More horses on the picket line. More fires. And at the eastern edge of the camp, set apart but not distant, a smaller cluster of shelters made of bark and animal hides where a group of Shawnee traders had set up. Colby could see their goods laid out on blankets — furs, beadwork, leather, things made with a craftsmanship that was different from the frontier work but no less skilled. Trappers moved between the Shawnee camp and the main camp freely, trading in both directions, the business of survival overriding whatever politics existed between the two peoples.

Skunk stood beside Colby on the ridge. His left arm

was functional but he held it close out of habit, the body remembering the wound even after the wound had closed.

"Big one this year," Skunk said to Colby. "Word must have spread. More traders, more goods, more gold." He looked at Colby's pack — heavy with pelts, the rawhide straps creaking under the weight. "You're going to do well."

They walked down. Founder trotted between them, nose working, reading the hundred-person camp from the ridge the way he'd read the sixty-person camp in December — with interest, without concern, the assessment of a dog who had been here before and knew the routine.

This time was different from December. In December, Colby had been new — a boy nobody recognized, walking close to Skunk, hoping the buckskins and the knife on his belt would be enough to make him look like he belonged. This time, people knew him. Whitley raised a hand from across the camp. A trapper Colby didn't know by name nodded to him — the nod of a man who had heard the story and was acknowledging the boy in it. A woman near the central fire pit looked at Colby and then at Skunk's arm and back at Colby, and the look said she knew what had happened and who had kept the old man alive.

Skunk's boy. The words preceded him. They walked ahead of him into the camp and made a space for him that hadn't existed in December, and Colby walked into that space and felt it close around him like the buckskins had closed around his body — not tight, not confining, just present. A place that fit.

The trading was good.

Colby laid his pelts on Burnett's table on the second morning. The table was bigger this time — longer, heavier, loaded with more goods than the winter gathering had offered. Burnett stood behind it with his son, the same sharp-eyed assessment, the same clean-shaven face among the beards.

Burnett examined Colby's pelts. The beaver first — twenty-six of them, thick-furred spring pelts, scraped clean, stretched properly. Burnett took his time. He turned each one, checked the scraping, rubbed the fur between his fingers. He didn't speak while he worked. His son watched, learning the way Colby had learned from Skunk — by standing close and paying attention.

When Burnett finished, he looked at Colby. The sharp eyes held something that hadn't been there in December — not surprise exactly, but the recalculation of a man who had underestimated a variable and was adjusting his math.

"These are better than what you brought in winter," Burnett said to Colby.

"I had more practice," Colby said to Burnett.

"Twenty-two pounds for the lot," Burnett said to Colby. "Gold."

Colby looked at Skunk. Skunk gave the single, small nod. The nod meant more than fair.

"Gold," Colby said to Burnett.

Burnett counted the coins. More coins than December. Heavier in Colby's hand. Colby put them in the leather pouch with the coins from winter, and the pouch was fat now, the drawstring pulling tight, the weight of it on his belt a constant, physical reminder of eight months of work.

He did the math the way he always did the math. The winter coins plus the spring coins. The total was more money than he'd earned in a year at L&M. More money than Wanda made in two months at the laundromat. The number sat in his head and pulsed, because the number was not just a number — it was Carl's inhalers and Wanda's rent and shoes for five kids and the beginning of a life that didn't run on shame.

If he could get home. If the portal opened. If the gap in the rock wall still led back to the storeroom. If.

He pushed the if away. The if was not useful today. Today the pouch was heavy and the sun was warm and the gathering hummed around him with the sound of a hundred lives, and Colby Utterback had earned his place among them.

The sky changed on the third afternoon.

Colby saw it first. Not because his eyes were better than anyone else's — because his brain was wired to see patterns that didn't fit, and the sky had stopped fitting.

The color was wrong. The afternoon sky should have been blue, maybe hazed with the thin clouds of a spring day. Instead it had a greenish-yellow tinge along the western horizon, the color of a bruise in its first hours, the color that Colby had seen exactly once before — on a television in the break room at L&M, on a weather channel segment about severe storms, the meteorologist pointing at a radar image and saying

When you see that color, you get inside.

There was no inside here.

Colby looked at the river. The Licking was higher than it had been yesterday. Not dramatically — a few inches, maybe, the waterline creeping up the banks. Spring melt from the mountains upstream. Normal, maybe. Or maybe not. The river had been steady for two days. Now it was rising, which meant water was coming from somewhere upstream, and if the sky upstream looked like the sky here, that somewhere was getting rain. A lot of rain.

He looked at the ground. The flat ground where a hundred people were camped. The smooth, wide, level ground that the river had made by flooding and retreating, flooding and retreating, over centuries. Mrs. Delano's class. Eighth grade earth science. The PowerPoint with the photographs of houses underwater and fields turned to lakes.

A floodplain is flat because the river made it flat. When the river floods again, the floodplain is the first thing that goes under.

Colby's stomach dropped.

He found Skunk at their camp on the south bank. Skunk was sitting on a log, whittling, Founder at his feet. The old man looked comfortable. Relaxed. The gathering suited him better in spring — the weather was warm, the trading was done, and the only task left was waiting for the last day and going home.

"Skunk," Colby said to the man. His voice was tight. "Look at the sky."

Skunk looked up. The gray eyes found the western horizon. The greenish-yellow bruise. The whittling knife stopped.

"Look at the river," Colby said to Skunk. "It's up since yesterday. A few inches. And it's still rising."

Skunk stood. He walked to the bank and looked at the water. He looked at the sky again. He looked at the flat ground where a hundred people were camped with their wagons and their horses and their goods and their families.

"The animals," Skunk said to Colby. His voice had changed. The relaxation was gone. "The deer. When's the last time you saw deer near the river?"

Colby thought. Yesterday he'd seen a doe and two fawns at the tree line above the camp. This morning — nothing. The tree line was empty. The birds were quieter too. And Founder had been pressed against the fire all day, curled tight, nose under his tail.

"They're gone," Colby said to Skunk. "The deer are gone. And Founder hasn't left the fire since morning."

Skunk's jaw tightened. He looked at the sky one more time. Then he looked at Colby.

"Tell me what you're thinking," Skunk said to Colby. "All of it."

"This is a floodplain," Colby said to Skunk. The word sounded strange in 1781 — a word from a science class in a world that hadn't been invented yet. But the concept was older than either world. "The ground is flat because the river floods it. That's what rivers do. The sky looks wrong — that color means a big storm, a bad one, the kind that drops inches of rain in hours. The river's already rising from upstream. If the storm hits tonight and dumps rain into the mountains, the water's got nowhere to go but down, and down is here. This ground will be underwater."

Skunk didn't argue. He didn't question. He didn't ask Colby how a fifteen-year-old boy knew things about weather and rivers that the trappers who'd lived on this land their whole lives didn't know. Skunk had spent eight months watching Colby be right about things he shouldn't know, and Skunk had learned not to ask how.

"We go to Burnett," Skunk said to Colby. "Now."

Burnett listened.

They found him at his wagon, going over the ledger with Margaret. Skunk spoke first. He told Burnett the sky was wrong and the river was rising and the boy had knowledge of weather that Skunk had learned to trust. Then Colby spoke. He laid it out the way his brain laid things out — in order, in facts, without panic. The sky color. The river level. The absent deer. Founder's behavior. The flat ground. What the flat ground meant.

Burnett looked at the sky. He looked at the river. He looked at Colby.

"We've camped this spot ten years," Burnett said to Colby. "The river's never come up more than a foot."

"It hasn't had to yet," Colby said to Burnett. "That doesn't mean it won't."

Burnett was quiet. He was a man who made decisions based on evidence, and the evidence was split — ten years of safe camping on one side, a strange-colored sky and a boy's warning on the other. Margaret looked at the sky. She looked at the river. She looked at her husband.

"The deer are gone," Margaret said to Burnett. Her voice was calm and factual, the voice of a woman who had raised seven children on the frontier by paying attention to the things that other people ignored. "I noticed this morning. And the dog." She pointed at Founder, who was pressed against Colby's leg, curled tight. "That dog hasn't moved all day."

Burnett looked at his wagons. Three of them, loaded with goods — the inventory of a man who had built a business one pelt at a time and whose entire livelihood was sitting on flat ground next to a rising river. Moving the wagons to the ridge would take hours. If the boy was wrong, it was wasted effort. If the boy was right, it was everything.

"We move," Burnett said. He said it the way Skunk said things — as a decision already made, the words just catching up. He turned to his son. "Get the horses hitched. We're going to the ridge."

Burnett went through the camp. Skunk went with him. They told every family, every trapper, every trader. The sky. The river. The boy's warning. Move to the ridge. Move now.

Some listened. Burnett's word carried weight — the man didn't panic, didn't exaggerate, didn't tell people things that weren't true. If Burnett was moving his wagons, there was a reason. Thirty or forty people started packing. Horses were hitched. Shelters were struck. Goods were loaded.

Some didn't listen. The sky looked strange, they admitted. The river was up a little. But it had looked strange before and nothing had happened, and the river came up every spring, and moving a camp was hard work and they were tired and they'd been camped here ten years and nothing had flooded yet.

Colby recognized the math. It was Wanda's math — the math of people who had been getting by for so long that getting by felt like a system, and systems don't fail because they haven't failed yet. The math said: it's always been fine. The math was wrong, but the math was comfortable, and comfortable was hard to argue with.

By dusk, the camp was split. Forty people on the ridge, their shelters hastily rebuilt, their wagons parked on high ground, their fires burning against the darkening sky. Sixty people still on the flat ground, bedding down for the night, the river ten feet from the nearest shelter and rising.

The Shawnee traders were gone. They had packed and left without a word hours ago, moving upstream toward higher ground. Colby noticed their empty camp — the bare patches of trampled grass where their shelters had been — and the absence confirmed everything. The Shawnee didn't need a boy from the future to tell them what the sky meant. They already knew.

Colby stood on the ridge and looked down at the river bottom. The greenish-yellow sky had deepened to something darker — a heavy, swollen gray-green that pressed down on the treetops like a lid. The air was still. Not calm-still. Waiting-still. The still that comes before the thing that breaks the stillness.

Founder pressed against his leg. Skunk stood beside him. Below them, the river ran higher than it had all day, the water brown and churning with debris from upstream.

"How bad?" Skunk asked Colby.

Colby looked at the sky. He looked at the river. He thought about Mrs. Delano's PowerPoint. The photographs. The houses underwater. The fields turned to lakes.

"Bad," Colby said to Skunk.

The first raindrop hit his face. Then another. Then the sky opened.

Chapter Twelve - The Flood

The rain was not rain.

It was something heavier, something with weight and intent, as if the sky had been holding its breath for days and had finally decided to let go of everything at once. The drops were fat and cold and came so fast that within a minute Colby couldn't see the river bottom below the ridge. The world dissolved into water and noise — the hammering of rain on leaves and earth and the canvas of the shelters on the ridge, the rising roar of the river, and beneath it all a deeper sound, a sound Colby felt in his chest more than heard, the sound of the land itself absorbing more water than it could hold.

The people on the ridge huddled under shelters and wagon beds. Fires hissed and died. Horses stamped and pulled at their tethers, their eyes wide. Children cried. Adults spoke in tight, controlled voices that were trying not to become shouts. The ridge was high enough — thirty feet above the river bottom — but the rain was so heavy and the darkness so complete that height felt like a guess, and guesses were not comforting.

Colby stood at the edge of the ridge and looked down. He couldn't see much. The rain turned the air gray. But he could hear. He could hear the river, and the river sounded wrong. Not the steady murmur of the Licking that he'd been listening to for three days. A different sound — deeper, louder, the sound of water moving fast and moving heavy, the sound of a river that had stopped being a river and had become something else.

Skunk was beside him. The old man's face was hard in the darkness, the gray beard streaming with rain, his good hand gripping Colby's shoulder.

"There's sixty people down there," Skunk said to Colby.

Colby knew. He could see the faint orange glow of fires still burning on the river bottom — fires that were fighting the rain and losing, fires that belonged to people who had bet their lives on ten years of nothing happening and were about to find out what happened when the nothing ended.

The river rose a foot in the first hour.

Colby knew because he'd marked a stone on the bank before dark — a flat, white stone at the waterline, visible in the last light. When he checked it an hour later, crawling to the edge of the ridge on his belly, using a flash of lightning to see, the stone was gone. The water was a foot above where the stone had been. A foot in an hour. And the rain was getting heavier.

The screaming started at midnight.

Not one voice. Many voices. Rising from the river bottom like something being torn — the sound of people waking up in water, people who had gone to sleep on dry ground and were now standing in a river that had come to find them. The screams were mixed with the sounds of chaos — horses thrashing, wood breaking, the heavy splash of things falling into water that was moving fast enough to carry them.

Colby was running before he decided to run.

He was off the ridge and moving downhill through the rain and the dark, his moccasins sliding on the wet slope, his hands grabbing at branches and roots to keep from falling. He didn't think about what he was doing. Thinking would have stopped him, because thinking would have told him that running toward a flood in the dark was the act of a person who didn't value his own life, and Colby Utterback had spent too long in the hallway near the door to make that argument convincing.

But this wasn't the door. This was the opposite of the door. The door was about leaving. This was about going toward.

He hit the water at the bottom of the slope. It was knee-deep where the edge of the flat ground met the rise, and the shock of it — cold, fast, heavy against his legs — nearly took him down. He caught himself. He planted his feet and leaned into the current and pushed forward, and the water pushed back, and the pushing was a negotiation between a boy who weighed a hundred and sixty pounds and a river that weighed more than anything.

Skunk was behind him. Colby heard him before he saw him — the splashing, the cursing, the voice of a fifty-eight-year-old man with a bad arm wading into a flood because a fifteen-year-old boy had gone in first and Skunk would not let the boy go alone.

"Stay with me!" Skunk shouted to Colby over the roar of the water.

Founder was there too. The dog was swimming — not wading, swimming, his head above the water, his legs churning, his body carried by the current and fighting it at the same time. The dog had not been asked to come. The dog had come because his people were in the water and the dog's understanding of the world did not include a version where his people went into danger and he stayed dry.

The river bottom was a lake.

The flat ground where sixty people had been sleeping was under three feet of water and rising. In the flashes of lightning, Colby could see the shapes of shelters collapsing, canvas floating, wagons tilted and half-submerged. People were everywhere — standing in the water, pushing toward the slopes, carrying children, shouting names. The current pulled at them. The debris in the water — branches, planks, tent poles, barrels — turned the flood into an obstacle course, every piece of wreckage a thing that could pin a person or knock them under.

Colby waded toward the screaming. The water was at his waist now, chest-deep in the low spots, and the current was strong enough that he had to brace against it with every step. His moccasins found the ground underneath — still there, still solid, the river bottom that had been dry earth this morning — and he used it, pushing off with each step, his body angled against the current like a man walking into a wind.

He found a woman first. She was chest-deep, holding a baby above her head with both arms, her face white, her mouth open. She was not screaming. She was past screaming. She was in the place where the body stops making noise and puts everything into the one task that matters, and the one task was keeping the baby above the water.

"Give me your arm!" Colby shouted to the woman.

She couldn't. Both arms held the baby. Colby grabbed the back of her dress — rough linen, soaked, heavy in his fist — and pulled. The woman's feet came off the bottom. The current took her. Colby pulled harder, his legs braced, his body an anchor, and the woman came toward him and her feet found the ground again and they moved together toward the slope, the baby crying above them, the rain hammering down, the water rising with every minute.

He got her to the slope. Hands reached down from above — people who had already made it to the ridge, pulling others up. The woman and the baby were lifted out of the water and Colby turned and went back in.

He found an old man tangled in a collapsed tent, the canvas wrapped around his legs, the water to his chin. Colby pulled the canvas free with his hands — tearing, ripping, the wet fabric fighting him — and dragged the man to his feet and pointed him toward the slope. The man stumbled. Colby caught him. They waded together, the old man's arm over Colby's shoulder, the old man's weight pulling Colby sideways in the current.

He went back in.

A boy, maybe ten, standing on top of an overturned barrel, the water swirling around the barrel's sides, the boy frozen with the paralysis of a child who had woken up in a nightmare and didn't know the rules. Colby waded to the barrel and held out his arms and said "Jump" and the boy jumped and Colby caught him and carried him to the slope with the boy's arms around his neck and the boy's face pressed into his shoulder.

He went back in.

Each trip was harder. The water was higher. The current was stronger. Colby's legs were numb from the cold. His arms shook. His lungs burned from the effort of breathing against the pressure of water that was chest-deep and rising and didn't care that the body it was pressing against was fifteen years old and had been awake since dawn.

Skunk was in the water too. The old man worked the shallower edge, pulling people out where the slope met the flood, his bad arm tucked against his body, his good arm reaching and grabbing and hauling with a strength that the injury had not taken. Founder swam between them, the dog's head a small dark shape in the churning water, and once Colby saw the dog grab a child's shirt in his teeth and tow the child toward the slope, and the child was too scared to do anything but hold on, and the dog swam with the focused determination of an animal that understood the assignment.

Then Colby heard Burnett.

Not from the ridge. From the water. Burnett's voice, cutting through the rain and the roar, a voice that Colby had only heard in the controlled tones of a man who negotiated prices and managed ledgers and never raised his volume above what the situation required. This voice was raised. This voice was a father's voice, and the word it was shouting was a name.

"Thomas! THOMAS!"

Colby turned. In a flash of lightning he saw Burnett —
waist-deep, twenty yards out, moving against the current, his
big body tilted forward, his arms reaching. Margaret was on
the slope behind him, holding two of the younger children,
her face the face of a woman watching her husband walk into
a flood.

Thomas. Burnett's oldest son. The boy who had
worked the trading table beside his father. Sixteen years old.

Colby scanned the water. Lightning flashed again. He
saw it — a shape in the debris field near where Burnett's
wagons had been. A wagon was on its side, half-submerged,
its canvas top tangled in the current. And next to the wagon,
caught between the wooden sideboard and a tree that the
river had carried downstream, a figure. Arms moving. Head
above water, then below, then above.

Thomas.

Colby didn't shout. He swam. The water was too deep
to wade now — the flat ground was five feet under, maybe
more, the river reclaiming the plain it had built. He swam the
way Founder swam — head up, arms pulling, legs kicking
against a current that wanted to take him downstream and
add him to the debris.

The wagon was thirty yards from the slope. It took

Colby two minutes to reach it, and the two minutes were the longest of his life. The current pushed him sideways. Debris hit his legs — a branch, a barrel stave, something that felt like a boot. The rain blinded him. He swam toward the shape in the lightning flashes, each flash a photograph that he held in his mind until the next flash replaced it.

He reached the wagon. Thomas was pinned — his leg caught between the sideboard and the tree trunk, the current pressing both against him, the water at his chin. The boy's face was white. His eyes were wide and empty, the eyes of a person who had been fighting the water long enough that the fighting had used up everything and there was nothing left but the automatic gasp for air and the animal refusal to stop gasping.

"I'm here!" Colby shouted to Thomas. "I'm going to get you out!"

Thomas didn't answer. He didn't nod. He gasped.

Colby dove under the water. The darkness was total — no lightning penetrated below the surface, no light of any kind. He found Thomas's leg by feel. The leg was between two hard surfaces — wood on one side, bark on the other. The tree trunk had jammed against the wagon's sideboard, and Thomas's calf was caught in the gap. The current held everything in place. Pushing the tree away from the wagon meant pushing against the force of a river.

Colby pushed. His hands flat against the tree trunk, his feet braced on the wagon's underside, his back and legs and shoulders driving against the bark. The trunk didn't move. The river was stronger than he was. The river was stronger than anything.

He surfaced. Breathed. Dove again. He shifted position — put his shoulder against the trunk, his feet wider, his body lower. He pushed. The muscles in his legs burned. The muscles in his back screamed. The trunk moved. An inch. Maybe two. Not enough to free the leg, but enough to prove that the thing could be moved.

He surfaced. Breathed. The rain hammered his face. Thomas was still gasping. The water was higher.

He dove a third time. He found the gap. He put his shoulder against the trunk and he pushed with everything his body had — every muscle that eight months of chopping and hauling and trapping and carrying had built, every pound of strength that the wilderness had deposited in his arms and legs and back, everything that Colby Utterback had earned in the woods of Kentuckee since the day he walked out of a storeroom in Idaho.

The trunk shifted. Three inches. Four. The gap widened. Colby reached down, found Thomas's calf, and pulled the leg free.

He surfaced with Thomas. The boy was limp —
conscious but limp, his body surrendered to the water, his
muscles spent. Colby hooked his arm under Thomas's chest
and kicked away from the wagon, and the current caught
them both and pulled them downstream, and Colby fought it,
kicking, one arm holding Thomas, the other reaching for
anything solid.

His hand found a branch. A tree, still rooted, standing
in the flood with its lower trunk underwater. Colby grabbed
the branch and held on and the current pulled at them and
the branch bent but didn't break, and Colby held Thomas
above the water and waited, his arm locked around the
branch, his body an anchor between the boy and the river.

Skunk found them. The old man waded out from the
slope — chest-deep, his bad arm held high, his good arm
reaching. Founder was beside him, swimming, the dog's
body angled against the current.

"Give him to me!" Skunk shouted to Colby.

Colby pushed Thomas toward Skunk. The old man
grabbed the boy under the arms and pulled him toward the
slope. Colby let go of the branch. The current took him
sideways — two feet, five feet, ten — before his moccasins
found the bottom and he dug in and fought his way back.

He reached the slope. Hands grabbed him — Whitley's
three-fingered grip, someone else, pulling him out of the

water and onto the muddy bank. He lay on his back in the rain. His lungs heaved. His arms were rubber. Founder appeared and stood over him, dripping, shaking, the crooked tail wagging once as if to say: that was something.

Thomas was on the bank twenty feet away. Burnett was kneeling over his son, his hands on the boy's chest, his face a mask of the terror that comes after the danger has passed and the mind is finally allowed to process what almost happened. Margaret was beside him, holding Thomas's hand, her ledger-keeping calm finally broken, her face wet with rain and something else.

Thomas coughed. He turned his head and vomited river water and coughed again and breathed — a real breath, deep, the breath of lungs that had decided to keep working.

Burnett looked up. Across the rain and the mud and the chaos of a hundred people pulled from a flood, his eyes found Colby. The big man's face was raw with something that Colby had never seen directed at him before. Not gratitude. Gratitude was too small a word. It was the look of a man who had watched his son drowning and had been unable to reach him and had watched a boy reach him instead, and the debt that created was a debt that had no number and no currency and no payment plan.

Colby looked back at Burnett. He didn't nod. He didn't wave. He lay on the muddy bank in the rain with

Founder standing over him and his lungs fighting for air and his arms shaking and his body emptied of everything except the one fact that mattered.

Nobody had died. The river had taken the wagons and the shelters and the goods and the pelts and the flat ground where a hundred people had camped. But the river had not taken a single life, because forty people had listened to a boy and moved to the ridge, and the sixty who hadn't listened had been pulled from the water by a fifteen-year-old and a fifty-eight-year-old and a one-eared dog who refused to let the river win.

The rain slowed near dawn. The river held. The flat ground was a lake, brown and churning, and the things it carried — canvas, wood, barrels, a single moccasin spinning in the current — were the inventory of lives that had been rearranged in a single night.

Colby closed his eyes. Founder lay beside him. The dog's body was warm against his ribs, the way it was warm every night in the camp, the way it had been warm since the first night in the clearing when a stray had chosen a stray.

He slept. And the river, having taken everything it wanted, began to fall.

The morning after the flood was the quietest morning Colby had ever heard.

Not the full, breathing quiet of the forest around Skunk's camp. A different quiet. The quiet of a hundred people standing on a ridge looking at the place where their lives had been, and the place was a lake. Brown water covered the flat ground from slope to slope, still and heavy, the current gone now that the river had spread itself across the plain. The tops of the tallest shelters poked through the surface — a tent pole, the corner of a wagon bed, the peak of a lean-to that someone had built to last and the river had disagreed. Everything else was underwater.

People stood at the edge of the ridge and stared. Some of them had lost everything. Not almost everything — everything. Their pelts, their goods, their tools, their powder, the season's work that was supposed to carry them through the next six months. A man near the tree line sat on a stump with his head in his hands, and Colby didn't know his name but he knew the posture, because the posture was the same in 1781 and 2025 — the posture of a person who had done the math and the math had come up zero.

But they were alive. Every one of them. A hundred people had been camped on a floodplain when the river came, and a hundred people were standing on the ridge in the morning light, wet and cold and scared and stripped of everything except the fact of their breathing.

Colby sat by a fire that Whitley had built near the tree line. His body ached in places he didn't know could ache — deep in the muscles, in the joints, in the bones themselves, the ache of a body that had been pushed past its limits and was now presenting the bill. His arms were bruised. His ribs were sore where the current had slammed him against the tree branch. His hands were raw, the skin torn on his palms where he'd gripped the bark and the wagon and the trunk that had pinned Thomas's leg.

Founder lay beside him. The dog was exhausted — his body flat on the ground, his eyes half-closed, his breathing slow. The crooked tail was still. Even the tail was tired.

Skunk sat across the fire. His left arm bore the scar from Jenks's knife — a raised pink line from elbow to mid-forearm, visible below the torn sleeve where the river had ripped the buckskin.

The water receded by afternoon.

Slowly, the way floodwater always recedes — not retreating but settling, the excess draining downstream, the river remembering its banks and returning to them. By midday the flat ground was visible again, or what was left of it. The grass was gone, replaced by mud and silt and the wreckage of a camp that the river had dismantled in a single night. Canvas lay in muddy heaps. Wagons sat at angles that wagons were not meant to sit. Barrels had rolled downstream and lodged against trees. Tools, clothing, pelts, food — scattered, soaked, ruined.

People went down to salvage. They moved through the mud in silence, picking through the debris, pulling what could be saved and leaving what couldn't. The silence was heavy. It was the silence of people doing the arithmetic of loss, adding up the things that were gone and subtracting them from the things that were left and finding that the remainder was very small.

Burnett lost two of his three wagons. The goods inside — powder, lead, cloth, salt, the inventory of a trader's livelihood — were soaked or scattered or gone downstream. The third wagon, the one Margaret had insisted they park on the ridge, survived intact. Burnett walked through the mud where his wagons had been and looked at the wreckage and his face showed nothing, because a man like Burnett could not afford to show what he felt in front of a hundred people who were looking to him for what came next.

But his son was alive. Thomas was on the ridge, wrapped in a blanket, his leg bruised and swollen where the wagon had pinned it, but breathing. Alive. Breathing. And Burnett, who measured the world in ledgers and weights and the hard currency of goods exchanged, knew that the surviving wagon held a fraction of what he'd brought and that his son's life was worth more than every wagon he'd ever owned.

The council met that evening.

Not a formal council — there was no building, no table, no authority except the authority of people who had survived something together and needed to decide what happened next. They gathered near the tree line on the ridge, thirty or forty of the senior trappers and traders, Burnett in the center because Burnett was always in the center when decisions needed making.

Colby was not invited. He sat by his fire with Founder and watched from a distance, the way he'd watched most things in his life — from the outside, through a window, separate from the room where the decisions were made. Skunk was at the council. Whitley was at the council. Colby was fifteen and fifteen-year-olds didn't sit in councils, not in 1781 and not in 2025.

The council lasted an hour. Voices rose and fell. Colby couldn't hear the words, but he could read the body language the way he read tracks — the gestures, the head shakes, the nods, the moment when Burnett spoke and the other men went quiet, because Burnett speaking meant the decision was being made.

Skunk came back to the fire. He sat down on his log. He looked at Colby across the flames.

"They want to see you," Skunk said to Colby.

"Who?" Colby asked Skunk.

"Everybody."

Colby walked to the council.

Founder walked with him. The dog had not left his side since the flood, the bond between them tightened by the night in the water, the hours of swimming and pulling and refusing to let the river take what was theirs.

The trappers and traders stood in a rough circle near the tree line. Their faces were lit by a fire in the center — orange, flickering, the light catching the lines and scars and beards of men who had lived hard lives in hard country and had just been reminded how hard the country could be.

Burnett stood at the front. Beside him was Margaret, and beside Margaret was Thomas, standing on his bruised leg, his face pale but his eyes open. The rest of the Burnett family stood behind them — the six younger children, clean and dry, the children who had been on the ridge because their father had listened to a boy.

Burnett looked at Colby. The raw look from the night before was still there, but controlled now, managed by the discipline of a man who did his feeling in private and his speaking in public.

"This boy," Burnett said to the gathering. His voice carried the way it carried across a trading table — clear, unhurried, accustomed to being heard. "This boy saw the flood before it came. He read the sky and the river and the ground and he told us to move. Some of us listened. Some didn't. The ones who listened are dry this morning. The ones who didn't are alive this morning because this boy went into the water in the dark and pulled them out."

The circle was silent. The fire popped. Founder sat at Colby's feet and looked at the assembly with the expression of a dog attending a formal event and finding the proceedings acceptable.

"My son is alive because of this boy," Burnett said to the gathering. His voice changed on the word son — a fracture, small, quickly sealed, the crack in a wall that reveals what's behind it. "Thomas was pinned under a wagon in five feet of water. This boy swam thirty yards in the dark, dove three times, moved a tree trunk with his bare hands, and pulled my son free. He carried him to the bank. He saved his life."

Burnett paused. He reached behind him. Margaret handed him something — a leather satchel, dark brown, the size of a loaf of bread, with a buckle strap and a weight to it that Colby could see in the way Burnett's hand adjusted when he took it.

"The gathering has taken a collection," Burnett said to Colby. He spoke directly to the boy now, not to the circle. "Every man and woman here put in. Gold, coin, dust. What they had. What they could spare. Some gave more than they could spare, because their lives are worth more than their gold, and you gave them their lives."

He held the satchel out to Colby.

"This is not payment," Burnett said to Colby. "You cannot pay a man for what you did. This is tribute. From every person at this gathering to the boy who saw the river coming and went into it when he didn't have to."

Colby looked at the satchel. The leather was dark and the buckle was brass and the weight of it was visible in the way Burnett held it — three pounds, maybe four, the weight of gold coins and gold dust gathered from a hundred people who had survived a flood because a fifteen-year-old boy from Idaho had paid attention in earth science class.

He didn't reach for it. His hands stayed at his sides. Not because he didn't want it — the math was already running, the automatic calculation of what gold weighed and what gold was worth and what that worth could become in a house on Spruce Street in Corbin, Idaho. The math ran and the number was large and the number was Carl's inhalers and Wanda's rent and shoes and a car and a deposit on a house with enough bedrooms.

He didn't reach for it because he didn't know if he deserved it. The doubt was old and deep and had Arnold's fingerprints on it — the doubt that said Colby Utterback was not the kind of person who received things, that Colby Utterback was the kind of person who gave things away, who put twenties on a table that swallowed them, who worked and earned and handed it over and watched the number go to zero.

Skunk's voice came from behind him.

"You earned it, boy," Skunk said to Colby. The voice was quiet and rough and certain. "Every piece. You take it and you don't apologize for it."

Colby reached out. He took the satchel from Burnett's hand. The weight settled into his grip — heavy, real, the physical proof of a night in the water and a boy who had gone in when he could have stayed dry. The leather was smooth under his fingers. The buckle was cold. The gold inside shifted with a sound like heavy rain on a tin roof, and the sound was the most beautiful sound Colby had ever heard, because the sound was the sound of the equation balancing.

Not his equation. His family's equation. The one that had never balanced — rent minus groceries minus electric minus the inhaler minus the shoes minus the shame, the math that always came up short, the math that Wanda and Colby had been running since Arnold left and that Arnold had been making worse since before he left.

The satchel balanced it. Not forever. Not completely. But enough. Enough to stop the bleeding. Enough to give Wanda a year without the math eating her alive. Enough to put Carl in front of a real doctor and get him an inhaler that didn't run out.

If he could get home.

Burnett extended his hand. Colby shook it. The grip was firm and held longer than a business handshake — the grip of a father who was looking at the boy who had saved his son and was saying with his hand what his voice could not say without breaking.

Thomas stepped forward. The boy was Colby's height, thinner, his face still carrying the pallor of a night spent fighting a river. He looked at Colby. He didn't say thank you. Thank you was too small and they both knew it. He just looked at Colby and nodded once, the nod of a boy acknowledging another boy, and the nod said everything that words would have gotten wrong.

Colby nodded back.

The circle broke. People moved, talked, returned to

the work of salvaging what the river had left. The gathering would end tomorrow. People would scatter back into the woods, carrying less than they'd brought, carrying stories they'd tell for years.

Colby walked back to his fire. He sat down. He set the satchel on the ground beside him and looked at it. Founder sniffed it once, determined it was not food, and lay back down.

Skunk sat across the fire. He didn't speak. He picked up his whittling. The knife moved. The shavings fell. The silence between them was full — not empty, not heavy, just full. The silence of two people who had been through something that words would only make smaller.

Colby put his hand on the satchel. The leather was warm from the fire. The gold inside was heavy and still. He thought about the table in the kitchen on Spruce Street. He thought about the twenty. He thought about the shame in Wanda's eyes.

The satchel was going to sit on that table. Colby didn't know when. He didn't know how. But it was going to sit on that table, and when it did, the shame was going to leave Wanda's eyes and something else was going to replace it, and the something else was going to be the look of a mother who finally believed that her son was going to be all right.

The fire crackled. Founder breathed. Skunk whittled. And Colby Utterback, fifteen years old, sat on a ridge above a river that had tried to take everything and failed, and held in his hand the weight of a life that was about to change.

Chapter Fourteen - The Pull

They walked home slowly.

The walk from the Licking River had never felt slow before — three days through the spring forest, the trails soft with new growth, the canopy filling in overhead. But this time Colby felt every mile. His body was still paying the debt from the flood — his ribs ached when he breathed deep, his arms were stiff, the raw patches on his palms stung when he gripped the pack straps. He walked anyway. He walked the way he'd always walked through things that hurt — forward, steady, without discussion.

Skunk walked beside him. The old man was quiet, quieter than usual, the kind of quiet that had weight to it. Not the comfortable silence of the trail. Something else. The silence of a man who was thinking about something he didn't want to think about.

Founder ranged ahead, then circled back, then ranged again. The dog's energy had returned faster than the humans' — the advantage of a body built low to the ground and a mind that did not carry events forward the way human minds did. For Founder, the flood was over. The trail was here. The trail had smells. The smells were interesting. The rest was details.

They reached camp on the third afternoon. Everything was as they'd left it — the lean-to, the fire pit, the pelt rack empty now because the pelts were gone, traded or lost to the river. The camp felt smaller after the gathering. It always felt smaller after the gathering — the compression of returning to a world that held two people and a dog after spending days in a world that held a hundred.

But this time the smallness felt different. This time the smallness felt like the right size. Like a coat that fits.

Colby built the fire. Skunk lowered himself onto his stump. Founder lay between them. The rhythm returned — fire, water, tea, the evening unfolding in the order it had unfolded for nine months. And in the middle of the rhythm, steady as a heartbeat, was the satchel. It sat beside Colby's pack near the lean-to, dark leather against the deerskin, and the weight of it pulled at Colby's mind the way the moon pulls at water — constantly, invisibly, rearranging everything.

The dreams started that night.

Not nightmares. Not the dark, jagged dreams of Arnold's fists or the hallway with the door at the end. Different dreams. Bright dreams. Dreams full of sound and light and the specific, irreplaceable details of a life that Colby had left behind and was beginning to realize he needed to get back to.

Carl on the couch. The wheeze. The thumb. The small body rising and falling under the blanket, each breath a negotiation between lungs that didn't work right and a world that required breathing. Colby saw Carl's face in the dream — the round cheeks, the eyes that were too large for the face, the way the boy looked at Colby when Colby came through the door, the look that said: you're here now. I'm okay now.

Mary walking the kids to school. Shirley's homework folder. Austin and Justin fighting over the remote. The kitchen table with the bills spread out and Wanda's hands moving through them, sorting, stacking, the hands of a woman who was trying to build a wall out of paper.

The dreams came every night. They came with a clarity that Colby's waking thoughts about home had never had — sharper, brighter, more urgent, as if the part of his brain that stored his family had been turned up to a volume that could no longer be ignored. He woke from them breathing hard, his hand reaching for something that wasn't there, and the reaching was new. In the early months, he'd thought about home the way a man thinks about a place he left — with guilt and sadness and the dull ache of separation. Now the thinking had changed. It wasn't an ache anymore. It was a pull. A direction. A force.

Something was telling him it was time to go back.

He didn't say anything to Skunk for a week.

He couldn't. The words were there — he rehearsed them at night while Skunk slept, arranging them, rearranging them, trying to find the combination that would say what needed to be said without breaking the thing he didn't want to break. Every combination was wrong. Every version of the sentence that began with

I need to go home

ended with the image of Skunk's face, and the image of Skunk's face was the image of a man who had lost a wife and a son and had spent twenty-six years alone in the woods and had finally, against every expectation and every defense he'd built, let another person into the clearing.

Leaving Skunk was leaving a man who had nobody else.

Colby worked. He checked the trap line, though the trapping season was ending and the catches were thin. He repaired the lean-to where a spring storm had loosened the lashing. He chopped wood, hauled water, kept the fire burning. He did the work because the work was real and the work didn't require him to say the thing he couldn't say.

Skunk watched him. The gray eyes tracked the boy's movements the way they always tracked them — quietly, missing nothing. And on the seventh evening after they'd returned from the gathering, Skunk set down his whittling and spoke.

"You're leaving," Skunk said to Colby.

It was not a question. It was the same voice he'd used when he'd said

You're the least prepared human being I have ever encountered

and

The camp is yours

and

Mine.

The voice of a man who saw what was there instead of what he wanted to be there.

Colby looked at Skunk across the fire. The old man's face was steady. The gray eyes were clear. There was no surprise in them. Skunk had known. Maybe he'd known since the satchel. Maybe he'd known since the flood. Maybe he'd known since the day Colby had walked out of the woods in sneakers and a polo shirt, that a boy who came from somewhere would eventually go back.

"I have to," Colby said to Skunk. "My brother — he's four. He can't breathe right. He sleeps on a couch and I count his breaths at night. My mother works at a laundromat and comes home with her shoulders around her ears. I have five brothers and sisters and none of them have enough and all of them need me and I have a bag of gold sitting next to my pack that could change everything for them."

The words came out fast, faster than he meant them to, the dam breaking because the dam had been holding for a week and the pressure behind it was nine months of knowing he'd have to say this and not wanting to.

"I don't want to leave," Colby said to Skunk. His voice cracked. Not much. Just enough. "I don't want to leave you. This camp is the first place I've ever felt like I was worth something. You're the first person who ever taught me that my hands were good for something besides carrying other people's weight. You stood in front of a knife for me. You called me yours."

He stopped. He breathed. Founder pressed against his leg, feeling the trouble in the air the way dogs feel storms.

"But Carl counts on me," Colby said to Skunk. "Wanda counts on me. They counted on me before I came here and they're counting on me now, even though they don't know where I am. I can't stay in a place where I'm whole and let the people who need me stay in a place where they're breaking."

The fire crackled. The forest was quiet. A whippoorwill called from somewhere in the dark, its song clear and lonely and persistent.

Skunk didn't speak for a long time. He sat on his stump with his hands on his knees and looked at the fire, and the fire reflected in his eyes, and the reflection was steady.

"I knew," Skunk said to Colby. "I knew the day you told me about the boy on the couch. The brother with the breathing. I knew you'd go back for him. A person who counts another person's breaths don't quit on them." He paused. "I just didn't know it would be this soon."

The last sentence was quiet. Quieter than Skunk's voice usually went. It was the voice from the night on the trail when he'd talked about his wife, the voice that came from the place below the frontier stoicism and the dry humor and the thirty years of solitude. The place where Skunk kept the things that could hurt him.

"When?" Skunk asked Colby.

"Soon," Colby said to Skunk. "I don't know exactly. I think the way I came in is the way I go back. Through the rock wall. Through the gap. But I don't know if it's there all the time or if it opens and closes, and I don't know what happens if I wait too long."

Skunk nodded. He picked up his whittling. The knife moved against the wood. The shavings fell. The motion was the same as always, but slower, the rhythm of a man who was doing something with his hands so that his hands wouldn't shake.

"Then we don't wait," Skunk said to Colby. "We go to the rock wall. We find the gap. And if it's there, you walk through it."

He looked at Colby. The gray eyes held everything —
the nine months, the fire-starting and the tracking and the
stabbing and the flood, the doe he didn't shoot and the buck
he did, the night Colby pressed his hands against Skunk's
arm and refused to let go. All of it, held in the eyes of a man
who had lost everyone he'd loved and was about to lose one
more.

"But not tonight," Skunk said to Colby. "Tonight you
sit by this fire with me and that dog and we don't talk about
it. We just sit. Can you do that?"

"Yes," Colby said to Skunk.

They sat. The fire burned. Founder breathed against
Colby's leg. The whippoorwill sang. And the night held them
the way the forest had held them since the beginning —
quietly, completely, asking nothing in return.

Chapter Fifteen -The Walk

They left at first light.

Colby packed the satchel and his knife and the leather pouch of gold from the gatherings. He packed nothing else. The pelts were gone — traded or taken by the river. The buckskins on his body were his only clothing. The moccasins on his feet were the second pair Skunk had made him, the first pair worn through months ago. He carried what he'd earned and what he wore and nothing more, because a boy who had arrived in the clearing with nothing was leaving with the only things that mattered.

Skunk packed a canteen and jerky and moved around the camp with the slow deliberation of a man doing a thing he had decided to do and would not reconsider. He checked the fire. He banked the coals — left, where the draft came from the right, the way he'd taught Colby to do it months ago. He looked at the lean-to, the stump, the pelt rack, the cold cellar that Colby had dug with blistered hands. He looked at the camp the way a man looks at a house before he leaves it, memorizing the rooms.

Founder sat between them and watched. The dog's ears were forward. His brown eyes moved from Colby to Skunk and back, tracking the activity with the attentiveness of an animal that understood something was different about this morning but could not identify what.

Colby knelt beside Founder. He put his hands on both sides of the dog's face — the patchy fur, the one good ear, the one bad ear, the skull warm between his palms. Founder's crooked tail wagged. The brown eyes looked into Colby's eyes and the look was trusting and complete and contained no information about the future, because dogs do not live in the future. They live in the moment of the hand on their face and the voice of the person touching them.

"You're a good boy," Colby said to Founder. "The best boy."

Founder's tail wagged harder. He licked Colby's wrist. The tongue was warm and rough and the gesture was the most honest thing in the clearing.

Colby stood up. He looked at Skunk. Skunk looked back. Neither of them spoke. The morning was too full for speaking. They shouldered their packs and walked out of the clearing, and Founder trotted behind them, and the fire burned low in the pit, and the camp sat empty in the early light, waiting for someone to come back.

The walk to the rock wall took half a day.

Colby had not been back to the place where he'd entered Kentucky since the day he'd arrived. Nine months. The forest had changed in nine months — the trees he'd stumbled past in confusion that first morning were familiar now, part of the map his brain had built, landmarks in a world he'd learned to navigate. He knew the ridge. He knew the creek that ran below it. He knew the stand of hemlocks where the ground sloped toward the sandstone shelf.

He walked the trail without thinking, his moccasins finding the ground the way they'd found it a thousand times on the trap line — quietly, surely, the footsteps of a boy who belonged in these woods and was walking out of them.

Skunk walked beside him. The old man had not spoken since they'd left camp. The silence was not comfortable. It was the silence of a man carrying something heavy that he couldn't set down, the kind of heavy that didn't sit on the shoulders but in the chest, behind the ribs, in the place where grief lives before it becomes grief.

Founder ranged ahead. The dog didn't know where they were going. The dog didn't need to know. The dog's people were walking, and the dog was with his people, and the mathematics of the world were that simple.

They stopped once, at a creek, to fill the canteen. Colby drank. The water was cold and clean and tasted like the Kentucky spring that he'd learned to read by the moss on the rocks and the lean of the hemlocks. He held the water in his mouth for a moment before swallowing, because the water tasted like this place and this place was ending.

Skunk drank. He wiped his beard. He looked at Colby.

"I want to say something to you," Skunk said to Colby. "And I want to say it here, before we get to the wall, because once we're there the moment will be about the going and I want this to be about the staying."

Colby set the canteen down. He listened. He listened the way he'd always listened to Skunk — completely, with the full attention of a boy who had learned that this man's words were worth the weight they carried.

"You came out of the woods nine months ago wearing shoes I'd never seen and a shirt with letters on it and you couldn't build a fire," Skunk said to Colby. "You were the sorriest thing I'd ever seen in these woods, and I once saw a preacher from Philadelphia try to befriend a porcupine."

The beard moved. The almost-smile. Then the almost-smile faded, and what replaced it was something Colby had never seen on Skunk's face. Not the gray-eyed steadiness. Not the dry humor. Something open. Something that cost the man something to show.

"My wife died twenty-six years ago," Skunk said to Colby. "My son died with her. He was eight. His name was Elias. He had his mother's eyes and he followed me everywhere and I taught him to track and to fish and I was going to teach him to shoot when he was old enough, but he didn't get old enough."

Skunk's voice was steady. The steadiness was work. Colby could see the work in the man's jaw, in the set of his shoulders, in the hands that were still on his knees because if they moved they might shake.

"After they died, I came here. To these woods. I came here because the woods don't ask you to talk and the trees don't ask you to feel and if you stay alone long enough the missing gets quieter. Not gone. Just quieter. Quiet enough to live with."

He looked at the creek. The water ran over the stones, clear and cold, carrying nothing.

"Then you walked into my clearing," Skunk said to Colby. "And the quiet stopped working."

Colby's throat closed. He didn't speak. He couldn't.

"You are not my son," Skunk said to Colby. "Elias was my son and nobody replaces a son. But you are the closest thing to family I have had in twenty-six years, and teaching you — watching you learn, watching you stand up, watching you become the person you were always supposed to be — that was the best thing I've done since they put my wife and boy in the ground on the Clinch River."

He reached into his pack. He pulled out something wrapped in deerskin — small, flat, tied with a strip of rawhide. He held it out to Colby.

"Open it later," Skunk said to Colby. "Not here. After."

Colby took it. The object was light in his hands. He didn't open it. He slid it into his pack beside the satchel and the pouch of gold, and the not-opening was a promise, the last small agreement between them.

Skunk stood up. He brushed off his knees. He cleared his throat with the roughness of a man putting something back inside that had come too far out.

"All right," Skunk said to Colby. "Let's go find your wall."

The rock wall was where Colby remembered it.

The sandstone shelf rose from the forest floor at the base of a ridge, gray and weathered, the surface rough with the texture of ancient stone. It was unremarkable. A wall of rock in a forest full of rock, nothing to distinguish it from a hundred other outcroppings in the hills of Kentucky. Except that nine months ago, Colby had been walking through a storeroom in Corbin, Idaho, and had stepped through a gap in this wall and found himself standing in a forest that smelled like smoke.

The gap was there. Colby saw it from twenty feet away — a narrow opening in the rock face, maybe three feet wide, dark inside, the edges rough and natural. It looked like nothing. A crack in a cliff. A space between stones. It did not look like a door between centuries.

But Colby's skin knew. The air near the gap felt different — a faint charge, a hum, something that was not sound and not feeling but somewhere between the two. The hairs on his arms rose. His body recognized the place the way a body recognizes the edge of a cliff or the surface of deep water — the automatic knowledge that the next step would take him somewhere his feet had not been.

Founder stopped ten feet from the wall. The dog sat down and would not go further. His ears were flat. His tail was still. His brown eyes were fixed on the gap with the intensity of an animal that was seeing something the humans could only feel, and whatever the dog was seeing, it had drawn a line that the dog would not cross.

Skunk stood beside the dog. He looked at the gap. His face showed nothing, because Skunk's face was built to show nothing when the things behind it were too large for the surface to hold.

"I can feel it," Skunk said to Colby. "Something. The air's different."

"That's it," Colby said to Skunk. "That's where I came through."

They stood there. The gap waited. The forest was quiet around them — the deep, breathing quiet that Colby had learned to hear in his first weeks, the sound of a world that was alive and ancient and indifferent to the boy standing at its edge.

Colby turned to Skunk.

The old man was looking at him. The gray eyes were clear and steady and held the full nine months — every fire, every lesson, every morning, every night, the knife and the blood and the flood and the stars. The eyes held the boy who had walked out of the woods in strange shoes and the young man who was standing here now in buckskins and moccasins with a knife on his belt and gold in his pack and the posture of a person who had been rebuilt from the ground up by the land and the man who lived on it.

Colby didn't know what to say. He had words — he always had words, the careful, measured words of a boy who thought before he spoke because speaking without thinking was a luxury he'd never been able to afford. But none of the words were right. None of them were large enough.

So he did what Skunk would have done. He stepped forward and he put his arms around the man.

Skunk was stiff for one second. The stiffness of a man who had not been embraced in twenty-six years, whose body had forgotten the language of being held. Then the stiffness broke, the way ice breaks on a creek in March — not all at once but in a single, decisive crack that lets the water through. Skunk's good arm came up and wrapped around Colby's back and pulled him close, and the grip was fierce, the grip of a man holding something he was about to let go of, and Colby held on and Skunk held on and the forest held its breath around them.

They stood like that. Five seconds. Ten. Long enough for the holding to say everything the words couldn't.

Skunk let go first. He stepped back. He cleared his throat. His eyes were bright and he didn't blink, and the not-blinking was the man's last act of control, the refusal to let the water fall in front of the boy.

"You go take care of your people," Skunk said to Colby. His voice was rough. Rougher than usual. The voice of a creek running over stones that hadn't been touched in years. "You go put that gold on your mother's table and you take care of that brother and you stand up straight and you don't let nobody tell you that you ain't enough. Because you are enough. You hear me? You were enough the day you walked into my clearing. You just didn't know it yet."

Colby nodded. He couldn't speak. The thing in his throat wouldn't let him.

He knelt beside Founder. The dog's ears came forward. The crooked tail moved. Colby put his face against the dog's neck and breathed in the smell of him — the warm, dusty, animal smell that had been the last thing he'd smelled every night for nine months. Founder's tongue found his ear. The tongue was warm and certain.

"You take care of him," Colby said to Founder. He said it into the dog's fur, quiet enough that Skunk might not have heard. "You take care of him for me."

Founder's tail wagged. The wag was steady and sure and made no promises it couldn't keep.

Colby stood. He looked at Skunk one more time. The old man stood beside the dog, his hand on Founder's head, his gray beard catching the light that filtered through the canopy. He looked like what he was — a man in the woods, a man who had been in the woods for thirty years and would be in the woods until the woods took him back. A man who had taught a boy everything and asked for nothing in return.

"Thank you," Colby said to Skunk. The words were small and insufficient and the only ones that existed.

Skunk nodded. The nod was small. The nod held the world.

Colby turned to the gap. The dark opening in the rock. The door between centuries. He shifted the pack on his shoulders — the satchel and the gold and Skunk's gift inside, heavy against his back. He took a breath. He took a step.

He didn't look back. If he looked back, he would stay. And he could not stay, because Carl was on a couch in Idaho counting breaths that Colby needed to be there to count, and the gold on his back was the weight of a promise he'd made to a family that didn't know he'd made it.

He walked into the gap. The rock was cool on both sides. The air hummed. The light changed — not suddenly, not with a flash or a sound, but the way dawn changes the sky, one shade at a time, the world sliding from one version of itself into another.

The dirt under his moccasins became concrete. The smell of the forest became the smell of cardboard and floor cleaner and the faint, stale hum of a fluorescent light. The rock walls became shelving. The sky became a ceiling.

Colby Utterback was standing in the back of the storeroom at L&M Food Center, Corbin, Idaho. The clock on the wall said 6:47 a.m. The date on the calendar beside the clock said October 17. His birthday.

He was sixteen years old. He was wearing buckskins and moccasins and a knife and carrying a leather satchel of gold. He had been gone nine months and he had been gone one night and both of those things were true.

He stood in the storeroom and breathed. The air tasted like fluorescent lights and linoleum and the specific, complicated, irreplaceable flavor of home.

Then he walked toward the front of the store, and the store was dark because it wasn't open yet, and the parking lot was empty, and the morning was cold, and Colby Utterback walked out the back door and turned left on Spruce Street and headed home.

Chapter Sixteen - Spruce Street

The walk home took eleven minutes.

Colby knew the route without thinking — left out of the L&M parking lot, three blocks on Main, right on Spruce, four houses down on the left. He had walked it a thousand times. He could walk it blind. But the walk had never felt like this before, because the walk had never been in moccasins on concrete, in buckskins in October, with a pack full of gold and a knife on his belt and nine months of Kentucky sitting behind his eyes like a second language he'd learned and couldn't unlearn.

Corbin was waking up. A pickup truck passed on Main, the driver glancing at Colby and glancing away and then glancing back, the double-take of a person who had seen something that didn't fit. A woman walking a terrier on the sidewalk stopped and stared. Colby walked past her. The moccasins made no sound on the pavement. The buckskins moved against his body with the familiar creak of leather that had been broken in by months of wear, and the familiarity of the buckskins against the unfamiliarity of the sidewalk was the most disorienting thing Colby had ever felt — his body in one century, his feet in another.

The air smelled wrong. Not bad — wrong. It smelled like exhaust and asphalt and the chemical sweetness of dryer sheets from a vent somewhere, and under all of it the absence of the thing his nose had been breathing for nine months — the clean, deep, layered smell of a forest that had never been cut. The absence was a hole. The world smelled like a world with something missing.

He turned onto Spruce. The houses were small and close together, the yards brown from the early frost, the driveways holding cars that were ten and fifteen and twenty years old. The house was where it had always been — white siding going gray, the porch light still on from last night, the front steps sagging on the left side where the post had been rotting since before Colby was born. The kitchen window glowed yellow. Someone was awake.

Colby stopped on the sidewalk. He stood there and looked at the house. He had seen this house ten thousand times. He had left this house a thousand mornings and come back to it a thousand evenings and never once had he stood on the sidewalk and looked at it as if he were seeing it for the first time and the last time at the same moment. The house was small. The house was tired. The house held six children and a mother who worked at a laundromat and a table where twenty-dollar bills disappeared and a couch where a four-year-old boy slept with his thumb in his mouth and his lungs working too hard.

The house was home. It had always been home. He just hadn't known what that meant until he'd spent nine months learning what home felt like in a clearing in Kentucky with a fire and a dog and a man who'd taught him that belonging was not a place. It was a thing you built.

He walked up the steps. The left one creaked. The porch light buzzed. He opened the front door.

The house smelled like eggs.

Scrambled eggs and coffee and the faint, permanent undercurrent of laundry detergent that never left the walls because Wanda brought it home in her clothes and her hair and her skin. The smell hit Colby like a wall — nine months of forest and smoke and animal hide replaced in a single breath by the smell of a life he had left yesterday and a lifetime ago.

The living room was dark. The television was off. The couch was occupied — Carl, small under the blanket, the shape of him barely visible in the gray light from the window. Colby could hear the breathing. The wheeze was there — the faint, high whistle on the exhale that meant the lungs were tight but working, tight but managing, the sound that Colby had counted for two years and had been counting in his memory for nine months.

Colby set his pack down on the floor. Quietly. He crossed the room to the couch. He knelt beside it. Carl's face was turned toward him — the round cheeks, the closed eyes, the mouth slightly open, the thumb resting against the lower lip where it had fallen out during sleep.

Colby looked at his brother. He looked at the small chest rising and falling under the blanket. He counted. One breath. Two. Three. The breaths were steady. The wheeze was there but it was the regular wheeze, the baseline wheeze, not the bad wheeze. Carl was okay. Carl was breathing. Carl was here.

Colby's hand moved before he decided to move it. He touched Carl's hair — lightly, barely, the touch of a person who had been away for nine months and was afraid that touching the thing he'd come back for would wake him from a dream.

Carl's eyes opened. The eyes were large and dark and confused for one second — the confusion of a four-year-old waking up to a face that was right and wrong at the same time, the right brother in the wrong clothes, the right eyes above the wrong everything else. Carl blinked. He looked at Colby. He looked at the buckskins and the knife and the face that was older and sharper and browner than the face that had left yesterday.

The thumb went into his mouth. It came back out. In.

Carl reached for him.

Colby picked his brother up. The weight of him —
thirty-two pounds, maybe thirty-three, the weight of a boy
who was small for his age because his lungs burned calories
faster than his body could replace them — settled into
Colby's arms the way the weight of everything had always
settled into Colby's arms. Naturally. Without complaint.
Except this time the arms were different. The arms had
carried deer and firewood and a boy named Thomas out of a
river, and the thirty-two pounds of Carl felt like nothing. Like
air. Like the lightest thing Colby had ever held.

Carl pressed his face into Colby's neck. The thumb
stayed in. The small body relaxed against Colby's chest with
the total surrender of a child who had decided that the
person holding him was safe, regardless of what the person
was wearing, regardless of the knife on the belt, regardless of
the fact that the person smelled like leather and wood smoke
instead of grocery store and laundry detergent.

Colby held him. He counted the breaths against his
chest. One. Two. Three. Four.

The counting was steady. The counting was home.

Wanda came out of the kitchen.

She was holding a spatula. She was wearing the gray
sweatshirt she wore every morning and the jeans that were
too big and the slippers that were worn flat on the left heel.
Her hair was pulled back. Her face was the face of a woman

in the first hour of a day that would be exactly like the last four hundred days — eggs, kids, laundromat, bills, couch, sleep, repeat.

She saw Colby. She stopped in the doorway. Her face froze — the muscles locking, the expression stalling, her brain receiving information that it could not file, could not process, could not reconcile with any version of the world it had been operating in thirty seconds ago.

Her son was standing in the living room holding Carl. Her son was wearing animal skins. Her son had a knife on his hip. Her son's hair was longer and his face was thinner and his shoulders were wider and his hands — the hands she had watched grow from baby fists to the hands of a boy who stocked shelves and put twenties on a table — his hands were different. Harder. The hands of someone who had been using them in ways that grocery stores did not require.

"Colby?" Wanda said.

She said his name the way she would have said it if she'd seen a ghost. Not loud. Not a scream. A question. The single-word question of a mother whose understanding of the world had just been broken and who was starting with the only fact she could verify — the name of her son.

"Hi, Mom," Colby said to Wanda.

Wanda looked at him. She looked at the buckskins.

She looked at the knife. She looked at Carl, who was pressed against Colby's chest with his thumb in his mouth and his eyes closed, already asleep again, because Carl had checked the only thing that mattered — Colby was here — and had gone back to sleep.

"What —" Wanda started. Her voice caught. "What are you wearing? Where — you didn't come home last night. I called L&M. Lloyd said you left at close. I was going to call — I was about to —"

Her voice was climbing. Not to anger. To the place past anger where mothers go when fear has been sitting in their chest all night and the relief arrives wearing something that makes no sense.

"I'm okay," Colby said to Wanda. "I'm here. I'm okay."

"Colby, what are you —"

"Mom." Colby's voice was calm. It was the calmest voice in the room, calmer than it had any right to be, the voice of a boy who had talked a man out of pulling a knife and had read a flood in the color of the sky and had held a woman and her baby above the waterline in the dark. The voice of someone who had been through things that the woman in the gray sweatshirt could not imagine and might never understand. "Sit down. Please. I need to show you something."

Wanda sat. She sat at the kitchen table — the table, the one with the bills and the twenties and the math that never balanced. She sat in her chair and the spatula was still in her hand and the eggs were burning on the stove and neither of them cared about the eggs.

Colby laid Carl on the couch. The boy didn't wake. The thumb stayed in. The breathing was steady.

Colby walked to his pack. He opened it. He pulled out the satchel.

The leather was dark. The buckle was brass. The weight of it was visible in the way Colby's hand held it — the careful, deliberate grip of a person carrying something that could not be dropped.

He walked to the table. He set the satchel down.

The satchel sat on the kitchen table. It sat where the twenty-dollar bills sat. It sat where the shame sat. It sat in the exact center of the equation that had never balanced, the equation of rent and groceries and electricity and inhalers and shoes and a mother who worked forty hours a week and a son who worked twenty and the total was never enough, the total was always short, the total was always a number that meant someone went without.

"Open it," Colby said to Wanda.

Wanda looked at the satchel. She looked at Colby. Her

eyes were wet. The fear was still in them but something else was arriving, something that was pushing the fear aside the way dawn pushes aside dark — not all at once but steadily, inevitably, the light winning because the light was patient.

She set the spatula down. She reached for the satchel. She unbuckled the strap. She opened the flap.

The gold caught the kitchen light.

Coins and dust. The weight of a hundred people's tribute, the savings of two gatherings, the earnings of nine months in the woods of Kentucky. The gold sat in the satchel on the kitchen table on Spruce Street in Corbin, Idaho, and the light from the overhead fixture — the same sixty-watt bulb that had illuminated every twenty-dollar bill and every overdue notice and every night of Wanda's math — caught the gold and threw it back, and the kitchen was bright.

Wanda looked at the gold. Her mouth opened. No sound came out. Her hand moved toward the satchel and stopped. Her fingers hovered over the coins the way a person's fingers hover over something they're afraid to touch because touching it will make it real and real things can be taken away.

"Colby," Wanda said to her son. The word was barely a whisper. "What is this?"

"It's ours," Colby said to Wanda. "I earned it. Every piece. It's enough for rent for two years. It's enough to take Carl to a real doctor. It's enough for a car that runs and shoes that fit and a deposit on a house with enough bedrooms."

He paused. He looked at his mother. The woman in the gray sweatshirt with the flat slippers and the bills on the table and the shoulders that lived around her ears. The woman who had carried six children through four years of not-enough with nothing but a laundromat paycheck and a stubbornness that Colby now understood he had inherited, because stubbornness was the thing that had kept him alive in the woods the same way it had kept her alive on Spruce Street.

"You don't have to do the math anymore," Colby said to Wanda. "The math is done."

Wanda's face broke. Not the way glass breaks — the way ice breaks on a creek in March. The surface that had been holding cracked, and what was underneath came through, and what was underneath was a sound that Colby had never heard his mother make. A sob. A single, wrenching sob that came from the place where she'd been storing four years of exhaustion and fear and the specific, grinding shame of not being able to give her children enough.

She put her hands over her face. The sob became two sobs and then three and then she was crying, really crying, and Colby went to her and put his arms around her the way he'd put his arms around Skunk at the rock wall — the embrace of a person who had learned that some things couldn't be said, only held.

Wanda grabbed the back of his buckskin shirt. Her fists clenched the leather. She held on the way a person holds on to something they've been waiting for without knowing they were waiting.

From the hallway, a door opened. Mary. Thirteen, dark hair, sleep-creased face, the oldest sister who walked the kids and managed the mornings and carried her own version of the weight. She stood in the hallway and looked at Colby in his buckskins and Wanda crying at the kitchen table and the gold catching the light, and her face went through the same sequence Wanda's had — confusion, fear, and then the thing that replaced them, the thing that didn't have a name yet because it was too new and too large.

Another door. Shirley, ten, holding her homework folder even in sleep, the folder clutched to her chest like a shield. Austin, nine, behind her. Justin, six, peeking from behind Austin's shoulder.

They stood in the hallway and looked at their brother. The brother who had left for work yesterday in a polo shirt and jeans. The brother who was standing in the kitchen in animal skins with a knife on his belt and their mother in his arms.

Colby looked at them over Wanda's shoulder. His family. All of them. Four faces in the hallway and one on the couch and one in his arms. Six children and a mother in a house on Spruce Street at seven in the morning on October 17, and the gold was on the table and the equation was balancing and the oldest brother was home.

"Happy birthday to me," Colby said.

He said it quietly. He said it to no one and to everyone and to the kitchen and to the gold and to the house that was small and tired and holding everything that mattered. He said it because the words were true and because truth, Colby had learned, was the only thing worth saying.

Wanda pulled back. She looked at his face. Her eyes were red and wet and clear — clearer than Colby had seen them in years. The shame was gone. In its place was something that Colby had been trying to put on that table since he was thirteen years old and had never been able to afford.

Hope.

Chapter Seventeen - The Hallway

Colby went back to school on Monday.

He wore clothes from the Goodwill rack — jeans, a flannel shirt, sneakers that Wanda had bought with money from the satchel. Normal clothes. The clothes of a sixteen-year-old boy in Corbin, Idaho, a boy who looked like every other boy in the hallways of Corbin High except for the parts that didn't fit anymore.

His shoulders were wider. That was the first thing. The flannel shirt pulled across his back in a way that the L&M polo never had, the fabric stretched by muscles that had been built by chopping and hauling and carrying deer through snow. His hands were different — harder, the calluses still there, the knuckles thicker, the hands of a person who had spent nine months gripping axes and rifle stocks and the rough bark of trees. His face was thinner. His jaw was sharper. The crooked nose was the same — Arnold's parting gift, the thing that hadn't changed — but the eyes above the nose were different. Steadier. Quieter. The eyes of someone who had seen a flood and a knife and a man bleed and had not looked away from any of it.

The hallway was the same. Lockers, fluorescent lights, the squeak of shoes on linoleum, the low roar of three hundred teenagers moving between classes. The smell of the hallway was the same — sweat and body spray and floor wax and the vending machine near the gym. Everything was the same. The building hadn't changed. The people hadn't changed. The schedule hadn't changed.

Colby had changed.

He walked the hallway the way he'd walked the forest — eyes forward, shoulders out, weight balanced, his body moving through the space with the quiet, unhurried purpose of a person who knew where he was going and didn't need to explain it. The walk was different. The walk was the walk of a boy who had tracked deer in snow and faced a drunk with a knife and swum through a flood in the dark. The walk said things that the old walk hadn't said. The old walk had been small and careful and designed to take up as little space as possible. This walk took up exactly as much space as Colby needed, and the space was his, and nobody was going to tell him otherwise.

People noticed. Not obviously — not staring, not pointing. But the way people notice when something in a room has moved and they can't identify what. A girl in his English class looked at him twice. A boy he'd known since sixth grade said "You look different" in the tone of someone making an observation they couldn't explain. A teacher paused mid-sentence when Colby walked in, the pause of a person registering a change without understanding it.

Colby said nothing. He sat in his classes and took his notes and ate his lunch in the cafeteria — the free lunch, the same free lunch, the turkey sandwich and the apple and the milk — and the cafeteria was loud and bright and smelled like nothing that had ever grown in the ground, and Colby ate the food and missed Skunk's rabbit and the smoke and the fire and the silence.

He missed it all. The missing sat in his chest like a stone, heavy and permanent, and the stone was the price of coming home. He had known there would be a price. Everything had a price. Kentucky had taught him that. The pelts cost sweat and the gold cost a flood and coming home cost a man and a dog and a clearing in the woods, and the cost was real and the cost was forever.

But Carl had slept in a bed last night. Not the couch — a bed. Wanda had used money from the satchel to buy bunk beds for the boys' room, and Carl had slept in the bottom bunk with a new pillow and a new blanket and an inhaler that was full, and when Colby had checked on him before school, the thumb was in and the breathing was steady and the breathing was better. Not perfect. Carl's breathing would never be perfect. But better. Better because a full inhaler and a real bed and a mother whose shoulders had come down two inches made a difference that doctors could measure and brothers could hear.

The stone in his chest was worth it. Everything had been worth it.

Trent found him after third period.

The hallway between the gym and the science wing. The same hallway where Trent had delivered his daily assessment of Colby's worth for three years — the comments about the jacket, the shoes, the smell, the lunch line, the mother, the father who'd beaten him and left. The hallway where Colby had walked small and looked down and absorbed it and kept moving, because keeping moving was the only strategy that a boy without options could afford.

Trent was leaning against the lockers with two of his friends. Sixteen, held back a year, six feet tall with the kind of body that coaches recruited and the kind of face that smiled when it shouldn't. He saw Colby. The smile came. The smile was a reflex — automatic, practiced, the smile of a boy who had found a toy he hadn't broken yet and was reaching for it.

Colby walked toward him. Not around him. Not past him. Toward him. The walk was the same walk he'd used in the forest — steady, balanced, eyes forward. He didn't slow down. He didn't speed up. He walked at the speed of a person who was going somewhere and the somewhere was straight ahead.

Trent pushed off the lockers. He stepped into the hallway. He blocked the path, the way he'd blocked the path a hundred times — the big body filling the space, the smile filling the face, the voice queued up with whatever the mouth had decided to say today.

Trent opened his mouth.

Colby stopped. He turned his head. He looked Trent in the eye.

The looking was the thing. Not the stopping, not the turning. The looking. Colby looked at Trent the way Skunk had looked at Jenks — the direct, level, unblinking gaze of a person who had measured the situation and was not afraid of what the measurement showed. The gaze said nothing and everything. It said: I see you. I have seen worse than you. I have stood in front of worse than you and I did not move.

Trent's mouth was open. The words were coming. Colby could see them forming — the shape of the insult, the curl of the lip, the specific architecture of cruelty that Trent had been perfecting since seventh grade.

Colby hit him.

One punch. Right hand. Clean and hard, the full rotation of the shoulder, the weight of the body behind it, the mechanics of a strike that Colby had never been taught but that his body understood the way it understood swinging an axe — the transfer of force from the ground through the legs through the hips through the shoulder through the fist into the target. The fist connected with the left side of Trent's jaw. The sound was short and hard, the sound of knuckle on bone, and the sound filled the hallway the way a single word fills a silent room.

Trent went down.

Not staggering-down. Not stumbling-down. Down. His legs folded and his body followed and he hit the linoleum the way Jenks had hit the ground at the gathering — all at once, the weight of him meeting the floor with a sound that was louder than the punch because the floor was harder than the fist.

The hallway went silent. Three hundred teenagers who had been moving and talking and living their loud, careless lives stopped. The silence was total. The silence was the sound of a hallway recalculating.

Trent's two friends stood against the lockers. They did not move. They did not step forward. They looked at Colby the way Pruitt had looked at Skunk — the look of men reassessing the terms of an arrangement they had thought they understood.

Trent was on the floor. He was not unconscious — his eyes were open, his hand was on his jaw, his face was showing the specific confusion of a person who had pushed the same button a thousand times and gotten the same result

and had just gotten a different result and didn't have a
category for it.

Colby stood over him. He didn't say anything. He
didn't need to. The punch had said everything the punch
needed to say, and adding words to it would have made it
smaller. He looked at Trent on the floor. He looked at Trent's
friends against the lockers. He looked at the hallway full of
silent students who were watching him with the attention of
people who were witnessing a thing they would remember
and retell and that would change the way they understood
the boy with the crooked nose and the Goodwill jacket.

Colby turned. He walked away. His footsteps were the
only sound in the hallway. The moccasins were gone but the
walk was the same — steady, unhurried, the walk of a person
who had done what needed doing and was done.

Behind him, the hallway began to breathe again.

The principal called Wanda at noon.

Three-day suspension. Colby sat in the office while the
principal — a tired man in a short-sleeved shirt who had seen
enough fights to process them the way a mechanic processes
oil changes — explained the school's zero-tolerance policy on
violence. Colby listened. He didn't argue. He didn't explain.
He sat in the chair and accepted the suspension the way he
accepted weather — as a thing that was happening, outside

his control, the cost of a decision he'd already made and would make again.

Wanda came to pick him up. She walked into the office and looked at Colby and looked at the principal and signed the form and walked Colby to the car — a used Honda Civic she'd bought three days ago with money from the satchel, the first car the family had owned in two years.

They sat in the car. Wanda didn't start the engine. She looked at Colby. Her hands were on the steering wheel. Her face was the face of a mother who was trying to be angry and was having trouble with the trying.

"You hit a boy," Wanda said to Colby.

"Yes," Colby said to Wanda.

"Why?" Wanda asked Colby.

Colby looked at the windshield. The parking lot of Corbin High. The flagpole. The sign that said HOME OF THE BULLDOGS. The world that he had left and come back to and was learning to live in again.

"He's been saying things to me since seventh grade," Colby said to Wanda. "About my clothes. About our family. About Dad. Every day. Every single day for three years. I never said anything. I never did anything. I took it because I didn't think I had a choice."

He turned and looked at his mother.

"I had a choice," Colby said to Wanda. "I hit him once. I'm done now."

Wanda looked at her son. The son who had walked into her kitchen four days ago wearing animal skins and carrying a bag of gold and holding his brother like he weighed nothing. The son whose shoulders were wider and whose eyes were different and whose hands had done things she would never fully understand. The son who had changed in a way that overnight did not explain and that she had stopped trying to explain because the gold was real and the change was real and some things were true whether or not they made sense.

She started the car. She pulled out of the parking lot. She drove home.

She made him eggs.

Colby opened Skunk's gift on the third night of his suspension.

He had waited. Not because he'd forgotten — the deerskin bundle had been in his pack since the rock wall, and he'd moved it to the drawer beside his bed when he'd unpacked, and he'd looked at it every night since. He waited because Skunk had said

open it later

and later meant later, and a promise to Skunk was a promise to Skunk, and Colby had learned that the man's instructions were worth following even when the reason wasn't clear.

But three days was later enough. The house was quiet. Carl was asleep in the bottom bunk, his breathing steady, the new inhaler on the nightstand, the thumb in. Mary and Shirley were in their room. Austin and Justin were in the top bunk, tangled together in the way that brothers tangle when the bed is small and the bodies don't care. Wanda was asleep in her room with the door open, the way she always slept, the door open because a mother with six children sleeps with one ear in the hallway.

Colby sat on the edge of his bed. He held the bundle. The deerskin wrapping was soft — the good deerskin, brain-tanned, the kind that Skunk used for things that mattered. The rawhide tie came loose with a pull. The deerskin fell open.

Inside was a carving.

It was small — maybe four inches long, two inches wide, carved from a piece of dark walnut that Skunk must have been working for weeks. The carving was a dog. A dog with one ear up and one ear flopped, a crooked tail, and oversized paws. The proportions were slightly wrong in the way that hand-carved things are always slightly wrong, and the wrongness was what made it right, because the wrongness was the artist's hand, and the artist's hand was Skunk's.

Founder. Carved in walnut. Small enough to fit in a pocket. Heavy enough to feel.

Colby turned the carving over. On the flat bottom, carved in letters so small he had to hold it close to the lamp to read them, were two words:

Stay found.

Colby's hand closed around the carving. The walnut was smooth and warm from his palm. He held it the way he'd held the satchel on the ridge above the Licking River — tight, both hands, the grip of a person holding something that could not be replaced.

Stay found. Two words. The whole nine months in two words. The whole point of every lesson and every fire and every morning and every night — the tracking and the trapping and the standing and the flood and the blood and the holding on. Skunk had carved it all into two words and put it in a block of walnut and given it to a boy who had been lost his entire life and had finally, in a clearing in Kentucky with a dog and a fire and a man who gave his word, found his way.

Stay found. Don't go back to being lost. Don't let the world shrink you down again. Don't let the Arnolds and the Trents and the twenty-dollar bills and the shame make you forget what you learned in the woods. You were found. Stay that way.

Colby set the carving on the nightstand beside Carl's inhaler. The dog and the medicine. The two things that mattered most, side by side. He looked at them in the lamplight — the carved walnut and the plastic inhaler, Kentucky and Idaho, the man who'd taught him to stand and the brother who needed him to come home.

He turned off the lamp. He lay down. He listened to Carl's breathing in the dark. The wheeze was quiet tonight. Barely there. The new inhaler was working.

He picked up the carving and held it against his chest, and the walnut was warm, and the breathing was steady, and Colby closed his eyes.

The gold was enough.

Colby had taken the coins and the dust to a dealer in Boise — a two-hour drive in the Honda, Wanda beside him, both of them sitting across a desk from a man who wore glasses and weighed things on a scale and spoke in numbers. The man examined the coins. He examined the dust. He asked where the gold had come from, and Colby said it was an inheritance, and the man looked at the buckskin-tanned hands of the sixteen-year-old boy sitting across from him and decided not to ask a second question.

The number was forty-seven thousand dollars.

Wanda heard the number. She looked at Colby. She looked at the man. She looked back at Colby. Her mouth opened and closed and opened again, and the sound that came out was not a word. It was a breath. The breath of a woman who had been drowning in arithmetic for four years and had just been told the water was receding.

Forty-seven thousand dollars. Colby did the math the way he always did the math — automatically, precisely, the numbers arranging themselves in his head the way tracks arranged themselves on the ground.

Rent for two years: fourteen thousand. Carl's doctor — a real doctor, a specialist, the kind who didn't work at a clinic that smelled like floor cleaner and didn't have enough chairs: five thousand. The Honda, already bought: three thousand. Insurance for the Honda: two thousand. Clothes for six kids — real clothes, not Goodwill clothes, clothes that didn't come with another child's history in the fabric: two thousand. Deposit on a bigger house, one with enough bedrooms, one where Carl didn't sleep on a couch and the boys didn't share a top bunk: four thousand. Emergency fund — the money that sits in an account and doesn't get touched and means that the next time something breaks, the breaking doesn't break everything: ten thousand.

The math added up. The math left money over. The math balanced.

For the first time in Colby's life, the math balanced.

November came.

The house on Spruce Street was the same house but different. The porch step was fixed — Colby had replaced the post himself, the carpentry rough but solid, the work of hands that knew how to use tools even if the tools were different from the ones they'd been trained on. The kitchen had food in it. Not the careful, rationed food of a family stretching every dollar — full food, the food of a refrigerator that didn't echo when you opened it. Wanda's shoulders had come down. Not all the way — shoulders that have been around a woman's ears for four years don't come down all the way in a month. But they were lower. The muscles were learning a new position.

Carl saw the specialist. The specialist changed his medication. The new medication worked better than the inhaler alone — the wheeze was quieter, the breathing deeper, the small body spending less energy on the act of being alive and more energy on the act of being four. Carl ran now. Not far, not fast — but he ran, across the living room, down the hallway, his feet slapping the floor, his laugh the high, breathless laugh of a boy who had discovered that his body could do a thing it hadn't been able to do before.

The thumb was still in. Some things take longer.

Mary didn't walk the kids to school anymore. Wanda drove them in the Honda. Mary sat in the front seat and looked out the window and didn't carry anything, and the not-carrying changed the way she stood, the way she walked, the way her face looked when she thought nobody was watching. Thirteen years old and already lighter.

Shirley's homework folder was the same. The folder would always be the same — organized, color-coded, the armor of a girl who had decided early that order was the thing she could control. But the grip on it was looser. The knuckles were not as white.

Austin and Justin fought less. Not because the fighting was about anything real — brothers fought, brothers would always fight — but because the frequency of fighting that comes from scarcity, the snapping and grabbing and holding of boys who have learned that things run out, had been reduced by the simple fact that things were no longer running out.

Colby went back to school after the suspension. He walked the same hallways. He ate the same free lunch, because the gold was for the family, not for pride, and free lunch saved money, and saving money was a habit that Kentucky had burned into him as deeply as fire-starting.

Trent did not speak to him. Trent did not look at him. Trent passed him in the hallway with the careful, studied indifference of a person who had recalculated and decided that a different route was advisable. The hallway had been recalculated. The other students had recalculated. The equation that had defined Colby for three years — poor kid, beat-up kid, quiet kid, the kid you could say things to because he'd never say anything back — that equation was gone. In its place was a new equation, and the new equation said: be careful with that one. He's different now.

Colby didn't hit anyone else. He hadn't wanted to hit Trent. He'd needed to. The distinction was important, and Colby understood it the way Skunk had understood the distinction between hunting and waste — one was necessary, the other was cruelty, and a person who couldn't tell the difference would do damage in the world.

At night, Colby sat on the porch.

The porch step was solid under him. The street was quiet. Corbin was a small town and small towns go to sleep early, and by nine o'clock the only sounds were the distant hum of the highway and the occasional bark of a dog somewhere in the neighborhood.

A dog. Not his dog. Not a one-eared, crooked-tailed, oversized-pawed dog who stole moccasins and towed children through floods and pressed his nose against an injured man's cheek. Just a dog, barking at the dark the way dogs bark at things they can't see.

Colby reached into his pocket. The carving was there. It was always there — walnut, smooth, the weight of it a constant in his pocket the way the weight of the twenty had been a constant on the table. But the carving didn't disappear. The carving didn't get spent. The carving sat in his pocket and pressed against his leg and reminded him, with every step, every hour, every day, of a man in the woods who had seen a lost boy and decided to keep him.

He thought about Skunk. He thought about the man every day, and the thinking was not the sharp, desperate thinking of the first week back. It was softer now. Steadier.

The thinking of a person who holds someone in memory the way you hold a warm stone — not gripping, just carrying, the weight of it a comfort rather than a burden.

He wondered if Skunk was sitting by his fire right now, in whatever time the clearing existed in, whittling, the shavings falling. He wondered if Founder was beside the stump, nose on his paws, the brown eyes watching the flames. He wondered if the old man missed him the way he missed the old man, and he knew the answer, because the answer was carved in walnut and sitting in his pocket.

Stay found.

Skunk missed him. Skunk would miss him for the rest of his life, the way Skunk had missed his wife and Elias for twenty-six years. But Skunk would not regret it. Skunk would sit by his fire and whittle and check his traps and talk to Founder and live the life he had been living for thirty years, and somewhere inside the gray eyes and the dry humor and the silence, the nine months with Colby would sit like an ember in a banked fire — not burning, not dying, just there. Warm. Permanent. The evidence that the quiet had been broken once and the breaking had been worth it.

Colby sat on the porch. The night was cold. October cold, the cold of an Idaho autumn, the kind of cold that would have sent him inside a year ago. He didn't go inside. The cold was nothing. He had slept through January in a lean-to with a deerskin and a dog and a fire, and October in Idaho was a warm afternoon compared to that.

He held the carving. He looked at the stars. The stars over Corbin were fewer than the stars over Kentucky — the light pollution of a small town dimming the sky, reducing the thousands to hundreds. But they were the same stars. The same ones he'd looked at on his first night in the clearing, the night Skunk had fed him rabbit and pointed at the sky and Colby had seen more stars than he knew existed.

The same stars. Different sky. Same boy. Different boy.

From inside the house, he heard Carl cough. A small cough. Not the wheeze-cough, not the bad cough. Just a cough. The cough of a four-year-old boy sleeping in a real bed with real medicine and a brother on the porch who would come inside and check on him before he went to sleep, the way the brother always checked, the way the brother would always check, because counting breaths was what Colby Utterback did, and the counting was love, and the love was the thing he'd carried through the portal in both directions — into Kentucky and back out again — the one thing that weighed nothing and was worth more than gold.

He put the carving back in his pocket. He stood up. He went inside. He walked down the hallway — not the hallway at Corbin High with the lockers and the fluorescent lights, and not the hallway in his mind with the door at the end. A different hallway. The hallway of his house, with the worn carpet and the family photos and the light from the bathroom and the sounds of six people sleeping behind closed doors.

The door at the end of this hallway was Carl's room. Colby opened it. He looked in. The bottom bunk. The small body under the blanket. The thumb in the mouth. The breathing.

Steady. Slow. The breaths of a boy who was going to be all right.

Colby listened. He counted. One. Two. Three.

Then he closed the door, and walked to his own room, and lay down in the dark, and slept the sleep of a person who had finally, after sixteen years, found his place.

A Note from the Author

This book is about a boy who doesn't think he's worth very much.

If you know that feeling — if you've ever looked in the mirror and seen someone who isn't enough, someone the world forgot to value — I want you to know something. You're wrong about yourself. The same way Colby was wrong about himself.

You may not walk through a portal into 1781 Kentucky. You may not meet a man named Skunk or a dog named Founder. But the thing that changed Colby — the discovery that his hands were good for something, that his life had weight, that the people around him were better for having him in it — that thing is real. It's waiting for you. It might be waiting in a place you haven't looked yet.

If someone is hurting you, tell somebody. Tell a teacher, a counselor, an uncle, a neighbor, anyone who will listen. You are not the things that have been done to you. You are the person you're becoming. And that person is worth every fight it takes to get there.

Stay found.

— Jackie L. Smith

Staffordsville, Kentucky

Acknowledgments

Every book is a collaboration, even when only one name appears on the cover.

Thank you to the readers who took a chance on a debut novelist with more stories in his head than years left to tell them. Your support means everything.

Thank you to Jessica, whose cover designs bring these stories to life before the first page is turned.

Thank you to every teacher who ever looked at a quiet kid in the back of the room and decided that kid was worth the extra minute. Mrs. Delano's earth science class saved a hundred lives in this book. In the real world, teachers save them every day.

Thank you to the men and women of the United States Navy, with whom I served for twenty years. The discipline, the grit, and the understanding that your word is the only currency that matters — those lessons are in every page.

And thank you to the kids who are still looking for their clearing. This book is for you.

About the Author

Jackie L. Smith served twenty years in the United States Navy, followed by eight years in hospital administration for the State of Oklahoma and twenty years of civilian service supporting the United States Air Force. He holds a Master's degree from Central Michigan University.

After more than forty years of service, Jackie turned to the stories that had been building in his mind for decades. He writes thrillers, adventure novels, and fiction for young readers, drawing on a lifetime of experience in places where decisions carry weight and character is measured by what a person does when nobody's watching.

Colby Utterback: Finding His Place is his portal fantasy for middle-grade readers — the story of a boy who walks through a gap in a storeroom wall and finds out who he was always supposed to be.

Jackie lives in Staffordsville, Kentucky, where he continues to write every day.

Connect

If you enjoyed this book, please consider leaving a review on Amazon. Reviews help independent authors more than you know — even a single sentence makes a difference.

Thank you for reading.